THE SURVIVOR

THE SURVIVOR

DR. ROSEMARY H. COHEN

LICO Publishing
Los Angeles, California
2002

The Survivor

FIRST EDITION

LIBRARY OF CONGRESS CATALOGING-IN-PUBLICATION DATA
Cohen, Dr. RoseMary H.
    The Survivor/ Dr. RoseMary H. Cohen _ 1st edition
        p.   cm.
    ISBN: 0-9667361-2-5
    I. Cohen, RoseMary H.   II. Title.
    1. History 2.Migration 3.Womens' Studies 4.Middle East
    5.Widowhood 6.Single Parent 7.Armenian Massacres Survivors
    8.Biography 9.Family Relationship

UPC: 795808-41819
[BM]   200113117
                                                        CIP

        03 04 05 06 07 08   RRDH   10 9 8 7 6 5 4 3 2 1

*In the loving memory
of my grandmother,
Arousiak*

TABLE OF CONTENTS

Acknowledgments

After so many years I realize that the suffering the Turks, caused through their actions to our grandparents, affected not only the immediate victims. It has followed us for generations. The consequences of their actions have changed the lives of so many innocent people.

I have come to realize that this book was carved in my heart since a very young age. The day I decided to write, it took me only a month to finish it. I was surprised how my memories were pouring from my fingers. I have always questioned my grandmother and our relatives about their history, although I knew I was touching an open wound. I have collected my information, word by word, for many years as the survivors had forgotten how to make sentences of these atrocities. I felt that it was my responsibility to remember and remind the world of the sufferings afflicted to the population of a beautiful city named **Khoy**. This story has been stored in my mind all my life. The night I put the last period on my manuscript, I felt totally at peace. It seemed that a very heavy load was lifted from my shoulders. I was not aware how important it has been for me to retell this story. Now I feel I have given back just a small token, to my grandmother, in exchange for all her goodness and sacrifices.

Not many people are aware of the Armenian massacre that took place at the beginning of the twentieth century. Not many people know that the Turks did not stop their atrocities inside Turkey but continued their cleansing policy in the neighboring countries.

My aim in writing this book is not to reopen the old wounds or make a political statement. The purpose of this book is a human appeal, as it is said in Hebrew, "Zakhor" to remember. We have to remember the past history and the many innocent people who lost their lives and we should remember the survivors who suffered so much by such cruel acts.

I can understand that sometimes countries have political, economic and geographical importance that the others do not, but this should not be a reason to forget what each one has done or is doing. If we compromise for any reason we encourage the evil and welcome new atrocities in our society. I do not know where this quote comes from but it says:
" **The only thing necessary for the triumph of evil is for good people to do nothing.**"

Unfortunately many politicians, historians and authors forget to mention the Armenian massacre and this encourages some people to continue their evil thoughts and actions.

This statement of A. Hitler on August 22,1939 proves these ideas. " I have given orders to my Death Units to exterminate without mercy or pity men, women, and children belonging to the Polish -speaking race. It is only in this manner that we can acquire the vital territory, which we need. After all, who remembers today the extermination of the Armenians?"

We have enough information to see the result of such evil thoughts to humanity.

Recently I have been visiting different libraries around the country and was surprised at the absence of the recognition of the Armenian genocide (or whatever terminology one would like to use) in many books. In chronological books, where each year is shown in a column, where all the important political, social and artistic events are marked in by months and days. I was looking anxiously to find at least a word about Armenians in the years from 1910 to 1920, unfortunately I did not find any word about Armenia or Armenians mentioned in any of the columns. In another book, "Remembering to Forget", by Barbie Zelizer,[1] The author has forgotten to mention about one and half million Armenians but has remembered:

"Atrocities as wide-ranging as the liquidation of a reported two million Cambodians by the Khmer Rouge, Saddam Hussein's Genocidal actions against the Kurds of Iraq, acts of brutality against the Bahai in Iran, 30 million killed by intentional famine in Mao's China, massacres in Rwanda and nearly Burundi, mass barbarism in Bosnia, and killings in Algeria, add new leaves to our scrap books, each of which stretches further the cumulative sum of deaths of violence. No wonder, then, that the contemporary age has earned such dubious

---

[1]- Published by University of Chicago Press, Chicago 1998.

titles as "the age of genocide" and the most murderous century in history." [2]

In the book of "The Century" by Peter Jennings and Todd Brewster, there is no picture or a word about Armenian massacre. Both books talk about the century and they forget mentioning the Armenians. How can one forget one and half million innocent men, women and children?

I think by forgetting or denying a crime, not only we spread injustice around us but we kill the victims for a second time.

What is the reason? Aren't one and a half million people important enough to be mentioned?

In the Old Testament we read that when God decided to destroy Sodom-Gomorrah, it is written that: " Abraham stood yet before the Lord. And Abraham drew near, and said: " Wilt Thou indeed sweep away the righteous with the wicked? Peradventure there are fifty righteous within the city; wilt Thou indeed sweep away and not forgive the place for the fifty righteous that are therein?" God says no. He bargains till he reaches ten righteous persons. God again replies that if he finds ten righteous persons, the city will not be destroyed.

Well, I know of so many innocent children who were killed in the Armenian massacre, yet nobody protected them at that time and no one wants to mention them at this time. I know from my grandmother that there were many righteous and honest people in Khoy, yet nobody stopped the Turks at that time and nobody wants to remember them at this time.

I have no hate in my heart toward any nation or the actu-

---

[2]- page 203,ibid

al Turkish people. I am just hoping that by showing all the sufferings imposed on innocent people, events like this will be stopped around the world.

Unfortunately, the human violence follows us always, even in the Twenty-First-Century. Can one of the reasons be that for so many years we have neglected to recognize and condemn the past horrors?

It is my dream that the universal understanding and acceptance of human differences will finally occur one day soon. I am not asking for restoration of materials or money for damages. How much can the Turks pay us for the sufferings of my grandmother? What is the monetary value that you can put on my grandfather? How about all that my mother missed while she was growing up? How about the value of not knowing what a father is like, how he looked and how warm his lips felt on her cheeks? How about us, how much does it cost, that we never know how great it could have been to have a grandfather. How much do you want to pay us, hundreds of millions or billions? Human suffering does not have monetary value. You cannot buy a death with a green paper.

I am looking for the day that finally the Turks will come forward and tell us: "We are sorry for the pain that our past politicians have caused you. Let us remember the sufferings of all the victims. Let us work together for a better future, so that horrors like this will never repeat anywhere in the world." I am sure on that day the blood of my grandfather spread in the streets of Khoy and the bones of my grandmother buried in Teheran's Armenian cemetery will finally find real justice.

RoseMary H. Cohen, Los Angeles, California 2002

Preface

࿅

As far as my memory goes back, I remember a thin, tall, old woman with a calm, peaceful face and somber dresses. When I was a young girl, she was young too. But Metza, as everyone called her, (nickname for metzmama, meaning "grandmother" in Armenian) became an old woman at a very young age. Even the merchants and neighbors older than her would call her "grandma." She was the sweetest person in the world, always there to serve and to help. She never complained and never talked about herself. We never knew if she wanted or needed anything. Everything was always for others. She would save her pennies and later buy us candy or other gifts. She had few belongings. She had only a few dresses in dark brown, navy or black. When one dress would get too old, she would buy a new one. But she always dressed neatly, a belt at her waist to emphasize her trim figure. Even if she wore the simplest dress, you could see she had presence. She looked like a queen, but without a crown.

She was able to make the most delicious food out of

nothing. She would bake an array of cakes, *nazouks, dolma, khash, harrisa* [3]. Even when we did not have enough money, she would prepare delicacies for us. She would make a spicy spread out of garbanzo beans that everyone still remembers. She would mash the beans slightly, then add parsley, oil and walnuts. I have many friends who still ask me for the recipe. She made delicious jams, too. Her yellow fig jam looked almost transparent; her little green walnut, quince and cherry jams were luscious. She used to serve them to us on fresh bread with tea when we would return from school in the afternoon. She was skilled in making aperitifs, wine and the best pickles. Metza would hang fresh grapes from cords in our basement in summer so we could have dried raisins in winter. But most of the time my brother would eat them in advance. In winter we would see mostly dry branches hanging from the cords, and everyone would laugh at the naked branches. When we had a cold or sore throat, we would go to her. She would put Vaseline on her hands and massage our neck in a special way with her delicate fingers, and we would feel cured. My brother and I rarely needed medications. Metza knew everything about herbs, and she used them to heal us.

Early in summer mornings, she would buy white mulberries, freshly picked and packed in a wooden box. She would wake us up and say, "You have to eat them fresh, early in the

---

[3]- Nazouk, an Armenian pastry, made with flour, sugar, oil and vanilla. Dolma, stuffed grape leaves with meat and vegetables and rice. *Khash*, soup made of the beef or veal legs and garlic. Harrisa, made with wheat grains, beef or veal meat and water which is cooked slowly for hours, it is served with cinnamon powder and sugar.

morning, because they cleanse your blood." They were fragrant and sweet. She would never use much meat. Sometimes she was obliged to kill a chicken. In those days chickens were not so abundant in the market due to the lack of refrigeration. The butcher would sell them alive. When he had enough time, he would kill them and sell the bloody chicken complete with feathers. Usually men of the family would buy live chickens and do the killing themselves. Since my father traveled a lot, Metza would have to kill the chickens. It was so painful for her that every time she would kill a chicken, she asked for its pardon. "I am sorry to kill you," she would say.

My grandmother's life revolved around us. If we went to a relative's house, she would come along. Once a week we would go to her sister's house. Or her sister and her family would come to visit. On the first day of the New Year and on Easter, her brother's children always came to visit her first. Everyone loved and respected my grandmother.

Every year, she would go alone to only two events, which amazed me. On Holy Friday, the commemoration of the crucifixion of Jesus, she would go to the Armenian Church in the evening, before sunset. She would stay there awake all night. When she returned home in the morning, I would find her calm and peaceful. I knew she had cried a lot. But I was only able to see a holy glow covering her face. The other occasion was when the Iranian government would punish or hang a criminal in a public place. For many years in Iran they used to punish criminals in public places. In major cases where children were victimized, they would leave the criminals hanging in public squares for three days, to set an example for the rest of the population.

The Survivor

I would ask grandma how she could look at such horrors. "It was good to see justice served so the criminal would not be your neighbor," she said. I think she was looking forward to the punishment of the criminals who had destroyed her youth, from whom she never received an apology.

I would ask her about the war, about my grandfather and about her early life. "War is war," she would answer, "filled with atrocities. What do you want me to tell you? It is better not to talk about it at all."

For years, I tried to pull words, one by one, from her closed mouth. As a child I missed the grandfather I never met. We did not have a single picture of him. The few survivors remembered him as handsome and strong, rich and generous. Finally I painted a picture in my mind. But I never finished drawing his face.

I remember clearly the times when I was sick with a high fever. There was a wooden armoire in my room. I used to see the war scenes on its wooden panels with real people moving around. I saw mothers pulling their children to safety, men dying. Crying, I would call everyone at home and urge that we help them. It was an alarming sight to my mother. She knew I had a high fever. After putting a cold cloth on my forehead, she reassured me we were living in peace, that these scenes existed only in my mind.

My grandmother's name was Arousiak, and this book is the true story of her life.

&

PART I

CHAPTER ONE

Childhood 1899-1917

If I do not tell my story, our history will be forgotten forever. I do not want it to be forgotten. History should be told so its errors will not be repeated in other places.

I was born in 1899 in the city of Khoy, in northwest Persia. I was the second child in my family. My parents gave me the name of "Arousiak," the name of the last shining star that announces the beginning of the day (Venus). My parents already had a son. They were looking forward to a daughter. Between my brother and me two other children were born. But neither lived long. In the old days women would give birth to many children, but few would live. There were almost no vaccines or preventive medicines. My birth brought joy to my parents, and later another daughter and son were added to our family.

My father was an importer and exporter who traveled constantly between Persia and Russia on business. We lived in a small charming house. It had a garden covered with red roses that filled the air with their sweet smell. There were many fruit trees; the tallest one was a white mulberry tree that had the sweetest fruits in summer. Fresh water was always rippling in the garden. It was coming from a source situated in the heart of the nearby mountains.

My father was well respected in the town. After work the men would get together in the only teahouse in the city. They would exchange news and their views on politics and business, sip tea over little sugar cubes that they would hold between their teeth.

My mother worked hard all day. Four children in those days (and even now) were a lot of work. In order to bathe us or wash our clothing, she had to heat water on a wood-burning stove, as there was no gas or electricity in the city. She would sew all our garments by hand, and do all the cooking and house-cleaning herself. She even baked bread in the large, clay oven we had in the basement. She never complained. She always had a sweet smile on her face. Sometimes family members or neighbors would come to visit her. They would drink thick, black Turkish coffee. Later, they would turn the little cups upside down and one of the ladies would read the future of each woman with the help of the design made by the remaining coffee grounds in the cup. On the New Year or during Easter, my mother would cook nazouk, a special Armenian pastry. We would always sample the uncooked dough, although she told us that it would give us a stomachache. But we paid no attention.

We did not have many toys; mostly we played in the garden, intrigued by nature. We watched birds and insects, and we climbed to the top of the trees to gather and eat luscious fruits. I was a good tree climber as I was always following my older brother, Nicola. My younger sister, Zarouhi, and brother Aghasi would play together.

There was no kindergarten in those days. Our parents

2

and our relatives were our best teachers. Our grandmothers would tell us stories and sing Armenian songs. Most of the songs were somber and melancholic. But we were used to these songs. Sometimes I could see little tears falling from my grandmother's eyes; she would always answer that we had a sad history and that she would have preferred to live in the land of our ancestors, in Armenia. For us Persia was our country; we were born there and we loved it. We were aware that most of the population was Muslim and that we were Christians. But we accepted each other and lived peacefully side by side. My parents had many prominent Muslim friends who used to come to our house. We spoke Armenian at home, Persian and Turkish outside. All our family members spoke at least three languages. But my father also spoke Russian and French perfectly, and later my brothers learned Russian, too.

My father would leave us for months for his business trips, and one-day he would return with lots of treasures. He would bring us little gifts, small wooden toys and candies wrapped in shiny papers. After each trip he would tell us about our homeland of Armenia, its Mount Ararat and the amazing Russian stories of BabaYaga and his travelling adventures. In those days there were no telephones and the mail was inefficient. When he left us we would ask him when he would be back; he would always answer: "Leaving is in my hands, returning is in the hands of God." He was a very hardworking and devoted parent. We all would miss him a lot. After he left, we would cry and ask about him. But after awhile our mother's love would fill the empty place of our father. For our mother, though, life would become even harder. She had to do everything by herself. Then after a long time, the presence of dust and noises in front of the house would tell us father was back. We would run out, jump all over him and feel all the bags of goods and pet the horses and camels. My mother, with a large smile on her face, would watch us. I could see her lips were moving as she was saying her usual prayers, thanking God that he was back home safely.

We had a simple life. Our garden and house were secure, and they contained everything we needed. We were happy. Love and peace filled our home. When our grandparents would quote the Bible, I would always say, "Adam was sent out of Paradise, but we are still there. Look at our house and garden. What is missing here?" And they would smile and say, " We hope God will keep you and this place always like this."

Later the boys started school, but the girls had only half a day of schooling twice a week. It was a boy-girl society. Women were born to become wives and mothers. Boys were meant to be men and responsible. The girls just had to learn the alphabet in order to be able to read and write letters and sign their names. Nothing more was expected of them.

I loved school. I wanted to learn more than reading and writing a letter, but there was no one eager to teach me and the teacher would say, "You are going to clean, wash and cook and take care of your children. Why do you want to study? Just enjoy life. Soon you will marry and will no longer have the time to enjoy life."

When I was nine years old, there was a cholera epidemic in Khoy. Many people became infected and died from the disease. I caught the disease and became very ill. Later they told me that I was unconscious for three days. I did not eat or drink during that period. My eyes were closed and I

4

appeared dead. The only reason they did not bury me was because my body temperature was not cooling down, and Armenians bury their dead only when the body is completely cold. They covered my entire body and face with a white cotton sheet. I was put on a bed in the corner of the room waiting to be buried. On the third day, when my mother was again checking on me to see if I had become cold, she noticed that there was a little movement of the sheet. She pulled it off and, surprisingly, she saw that my eyes were open. After three days I was miraculously returned to this life.

When Nicola turned thirteen years old, my father told him he was now a man. He had to stop playing like a child. He must join the mens' circles and learn the family business. Suddenly from one day to the next, Nicola turned into a man. He would leave the house with my father very early in the morning, when we were all asleep, and return at night before dinner. He would go to the teahouse with my father and the other men to learn from their experiences.

My once joyous brother had suddenly turned into a serious person. My younger sister and brother continued to play and laugh loudly, but I, too, started pulling myself away from them and thinking about Nicola and his new grownup life. I missed him in my games. As a challenge, I would choose the tallest tree and climb to the highest branch that could hold me. From there I would look outside of my paradise, searching a new world. Maybe I was trying to see what Nicola was doing.

The Muslim women wore a *chador*, a large bias cloth that covered them from head to toe. The Armenians would wear their traditional costumes. The women would only go out when there was a wedding, childbirth or for a little shopping. Even the daily shopping was the men's responsibility. After Nicola's departure, my garden, which used to be so big, became small. My mother felt my sadness. She tried to comfort me by telling me Nicola should learn to become a man, that our father needed help, and that maybe I, too, could help her a little at home and look after my little sister and brother. She told me I should start learning about family responsibilities because soon I would be getting married. I told her I was still very young and I would like to study, go to school, learn to read and write, and then marry. She smiled sadly and said, *"Not in this country. We have to do what everyone else does."* I was sad that I would not be allowed to behave in a different manner than my closed society.

I started helping my mother with little responsibilities. She would never let me do hard work. Instead, she would teach me how to prepare some of her delicious dishes and pastry recipes. We would climb the fruit trees and pick fresh fruits, and then she would teach me how to make them into delicious jams. In a way, it was fun for me to help her cook. I would run out later to play with my sister and brother. We had recently learned a new game that was popular with children. On their last visit, my cousins had taught us "the bone game." We used a small bone from a lamb that we would throw on the ground. It could fall in four positions, one for each child's name. We would ask the bone to tell us, by giving the name of the child, what he would become in the future. And the answer would be hungry, full, beggar and king. It was fun. We would play this game for hours, and the person who would become the king would gain the respect of the others. We also used to have silkworms. We would

6

keep them in a box and feed them mulberry leaves, they would make cocoons and later a butterfly would come out of the cocoon and lay eggs. Sometimes we had yellow or white worms. The yellow ones were rare, so we would trade with our cousins. This would keep us busy for the summer. Later at dusk we would play hide and seek or jump ropes. We would draw chalk lines on the brick floor and play hopscotch. I had found the nicest stone for this game, and I kept it in my pocket. Sometimes when Nicola would return home early we would ask him to play with us. At the beginning he would be stiff and formal, as if he had forgotten how to play. But after the first game he would forget his new dignity and become a child of his own age. We would run around the trees and climb up and down.

A year passed. Now Nicola was asked to accompany my father on all his trips abroad. It was exciting. He was going to ride horses and see other cities and learn new languages. How I wanted to be a boy and do the same! The day arrived when Nicola kissed us goodbye and left for his first long trip. As usual, we did not have any news from the travelers. My mother would pray to God all the time and ask him to protect her son and husband from danger. Then one day the noises in front of the house would bring us good news. My father and Nicola were back from their trip. They looked tired, but happy to be home. My mother always brought them steaming hot water so that they could bathe and relax. I helped my mother prepare special foods for them while they told us about their adventures. Nicola had brought me a little wooden doll from Russia dressed like a character in a fairy tale and a small flat stone from Armenia. He told me he had picked it up from the Arax River. He said the water was so blue and clear that he saw this stone underwater and grabbed it for me. The stone had a soft surface and beautiful lines traced on it. I looked at it and I felt the pure water of my ancestors' river running through my fingers. I was so happy to have these precious gifts, and I treasured them dearly. After another trip he brought me a red glass marble, and he told me the tales of the Thousand and One Nights. He would tell me to look into the marble when the sun was shining, and I would be able to see Ali Baba and all the stories inside the marble. This little red marble became my new tool to discover the universe. After some time I started seeing all the old legends and stories that I knew in this little object.

My father and Nicola traveled much of the year. We became used to their trips and long absences. The departure was always sad, but the return was sweet. When I was ten years old, my father and Nicola left us again for one of their trips at the end of winter. This time it was different. My father kissed us twice. When they were leaving, we stayed at the front door longer and watched the last cloud of dust that was visible to our eyes. This time my mother did not rush us into the house. We stayed in the street, wondering when they would return. We all entered the house and spent the day calmly. My mother, as always, was hiding her tears from us and her lips were repeating the prayers for protection. I was very sad. Again I was not going to see my father and brother for a long time. I was thinking of all the dangers that followed them in their trips. I had heard that sometimes thieves would hide in the lonely mountain roads and rob or kill the travelers. Between Persia and Russia there were many villages and towns that had social and political unrest. There was poor hygiene and no medical supplies were available. The only bright spot was that the air, the earth and water were pure almost everywhere. Prayer was the main tool in bringing our dear ones home from their trips. My father and Nicola had guns to protect themselves. So I was reassured that soon they would be back safely, and who knew what kind of gift Nicola would bring home this time.

Time passed slowly and sadly. When I was in the mood, I would climb to the top of the tallest tree, squint my eyes and look far away in the direction from which their horses had left. I would imagine them sitting in a teahouse near Mount Ararat in Armenia, and looking up to its snowy top. The mountain has two bumps sitting side by side. They had told me the mountain looked like a sister and brother, and they would say that it looked like Nicola and me, one taller and the other smaller. They were protecting each other, and together they were watching over their country. I would imagine the Cossacks with their black uniforms and golden buttons. I would see the Russian women with big flowered hats and long *bouffant* dresses. All these were images that I had learned from my father and Nicola and now I could see them with my inner eye. I loved my family and country, but I wished I could have had the same opportunity that Russian women had, to study, to play music and to paint.

One day, when I was on the top of a tree, I saw a cloud of dust approaching our street. My heart started beating hard. I called my sister and brother, and I told my mother that I could see our father and Nicola in the distance. But soon I realized something was wrong. The dust was not as thick as usual. When we all ran happily to the door, we saw only one horse in the distance. The horse rider looked smaller in size, so we guessed that it was Nicola. We thought they were probably playing games on us, that our father was coming later. But I was sure I had seen only a little dust, and I knew something was terribly wrong. Finally the horse arrived in front of the house. My mother's face turned pale. She was stunned to see her teenage son alone, thinner and very sad. She asked him where her husband was. Nicola said he would come soon, and walked in. He did not kiss us, nor did he give me the little souvenirs he would always have in his hand. We all went in and sat around him, and suddenly I saw that my brother had become an old man. He had deep lines on his face and his clear blue eyes were filled with tears. This was the first time I ever saw him cry. We all started crying, as we knew something terrible had happened. He told us the trip went well as always. When they arrived at a city in Russia, while they were staying in the house of a friend, our father had become ill. He started having a lot of pain, then a high fever. He could not eat anything. He could only drink water. The doctor who visited him gave him some medicine, but nothing helped.

My brother said father was burning with fever for three days. On the night of the third day our father called him with his weak voice. Father put his hands over his head and blessed him. He asked him to have courage. He told Nicola the time had come for him to play the role of the father in our family and that he should take care of his sisters and brother. He said that Nicola had learned the business and that relatives and friends would help him continue. He said he was sorry to leave him alone in this foreign country. But he had been called. His days were finished on this earth, and he said Nicola should be brave. Father told him that he would always feel his father's presence no matter where and when. My brother started crying, begging father not to leave him alone. He was changing the cool cloth on his forehead, trying to lessen his fever, but there was no hope. He kissed his hand. He prayed, but there was nothing that he could do to keep him with us. Father asked him to bend his head. He kissed Nicola. Father said to kiss everyone for him and tell them that he would always love us. Then he closed his eyes and stopped talking. Nicola continued in tears: "I felt that his fever dropped. For a moment, I thought he was getting better. But I could not say a word any more. His hands dropped down, lifeless, and I understood that he had died. I kissed his face. Then I sat near his bed and cried aloud. I was sad to lose him; I was terrified to be left alone. I was burdened with the responsibility of continuing my life alone. Suddenly, between my tears, I saw his sweet smile and I heard him saying, "I am ready for this. God will be with me, and he will protect us."

Nicola continued with his account. "I had never seen a death and had not dealt with funerals. Our friends helped me with this task. We buried father on a very cold and dark day in a Russian cemetery. It was raining. Even God was crying for us. My tears and the rain accompanied our father on his new trip. On a wooden cross we wrote his name. We placed the cross in the wet earth, which was holding his body. Immediately afterward, I decided to return home."

We were all crying and trying to comfort each other at the same time. We were aware that the peace of our garden had been shattered forever, and I felt that once again God had thrown Adam out of Paradise. My mother held her tired son in her arms and comforted him. But her eyes were wet with tears, and I could see the anguish on her face.

For days family members and friends came to visit us, to

cry and to remember our father with us. We served lunches and dinners to everyone. They drank tea and Turkish coffee, accompanied with *halva* and black dates. My mother wore a black dress and stayed calm, but in tears.

Soon our life started to return to its daily routine. Now Nicola left early in the morning for work. He came home earlier to help us as much as he could. After a year he started to travel again. It seemed he had really learned the business and was doing well for such a young man. Of course, our uncles and friends were helping him, but he was a very intelligent and capable. We were so proud of him.

Nicola became a successful businessman and had grown quite handsome. In his work he was dealing with a well-known businessman who had five children, three sons and two daughters. The businessman's wife was one of the more advanced women of the city. She had traveled to England and belonged to the Adventist Church. Armenians are Gregorian by religion. When *Grikor Lousavorich* came to Armenia in the year 301 to bring Christianity, he was the first follower of Jesus to spread his words to the world. The Armenian King Tertat put him in a dungeon and kept him there for a long time. One day the king became ill, and none of his doctors were able to cure him. One morning the queen woke up and told her husband she had seen Grikor in her dreams. She said it was revealed to her that he was a holy man, the only one able to cure him. The king ordered his freedom on the condition that he be cured of his illness. Grikor entered the palace and healed the dying king. The king freed him and gave him the title of *Sourp (saint)*.

From this moment, Armenia was announced to be the first Christian country among all the nations who were either

12

Zoroastrians or idolaters. The Armenians were Christians and Gregorian, which is closer to Greek Orthodox. The followers are completely devoted to Christ. Mary is considered only as the mother of Jesus, rather than an important figure, as in Catholicism. They do not have to confess every week to the priest. However, there is a community confession rather than an individual one. The thirty-first of December is known to be the date of the birth of Christ, so the year starts with his birth. The sixth of January corresponds to his baptism. Therefore on this day we go to church and witness the baptism of the cross. Everyone returns home with a little bottle of sacred water that is used for healing illnesses and for purification of the spirit.

The Armenian priest does not have total importance and authority in the country. He is the messenger of God, the one person who has studied the Bible more than anyone else. He is the one who will go from house to house after January sixth and after Easter to bless the families and their houses. He will listen to peoples' problems and solve their differences. He is more like a big father to all. He stays away from politics, but plays an important role in teaching the Armenian language and religion to the students, in order to perpetuate their traditions. On Easter everyone will go to church to listen to the prayers. Meanwhile, the children will play with colorful eggs decorated with dyes from onionskins and colored papers and flowers. Sometimes they return home with a lot of broken eggs. They keep the nicest one and eat the rest each day with *nazouk* and *paska*.[4] Sometimes the rest of the eggs are given to the poor or to a child who

---

[4]- A special pastry baked only during Easter.

lost all his eggs.

When I was about eleven years old, we all went to the annual community picnic with all the other families of our city and the surrounding villages to Sourp Sarkis Church. This is an oldest church built in a pretty valley. This picnic was held on the occasion of the Ascension. This corresponds to the day Christ was elevated to Heaven, promising he would return one day to establish peace on earth. For the Armenians (and I think for all nations), this is a very hopeful promise. Everyone looks forward to this day that will end all of our sufferings. The community used the occasion for meeting girls and boys from distant towns and villages, and it was one of the places where matchmakers would pick out future brides and grooms-to-be. Nicola was introduced to a beautiful girl at this picnic.

Nicola liked the girl he met. She was beautiful and tall, the daughter of a man with whom Nicola had worked very closely. Time passed and Nicola asked our mother's permission to marry her. My mother agreed happily. She thanked him for all his sacrifices and help with our family since the death of our father. She approved of this union.

My mother and Nicola met the parents of the bride-to-be and asked for her hand. Vartouhi was her name. We nicknamed his bride *Kharse*, meaning bride, and this name stayed with her forever. Her parents agreed, and they were happy to have such a responsible, successful and handsome man as their new son-in- law. In my mother's house we were getting ready for the wedding celebration. Finally my older brother got married. We had invited a lot of people. It was a big party, and we all had a very joyous time. Nicola and his wife moved into our house, in rooms added to the existing building for the new couple.

We were all living happily together. Nicola continued to be successful, and after his marriage he traveled to Russia often.

Kharse was a modern girl. She had become a main source of information for me about the large world I yearned for. She would tell me about all the experiences her mother had while living in England. She said that there was a long metal "house" that ran underground, and people traveled in it to go to work. She told us that women went to school and participated in many activities. They even had queens as rulers. We have also had Armenian queens in our history. But in our new country, women were veiled and stayed in the shadow of their husbands. Kharse was not like us. She would ask questions and impose ideas on her husband. We would all say quietly this was Nicola's fault, that he was a weak man for letting her speak up so boldly. But I knew better. She was intelligent and she was not as emotional as we were. Her brain always ruled over her actions.

A year after their wedding, Kharse became pregnant and bore a little girl. She was a beautiful baby. We had a big party for her baptism. The priest and many guests came for the ceremony. The baby, whose name was Lusine, meaning moon, gave us great joy. For me it was like having a real doll to play with.

One day Nicola, Kharse and her parents went for a short trip to Armavil, a city far from us. When they returned, I heard them talking to my mother. They said they had met Yeprem who had finished his studying in Armavil. He was from Khoy, and his parents lived in our city. He was known to be very intelligent, a good person. When they had spoken to him, he had said he was looking for a girl to marry. Kharse's father had said, "If you are looking for a good girl, Nicola's sister is the best candidate for you. She is beautiful and from a good family." I overheard this conversation, but I did not understand the real significance. I forgot all about it, never realizing how my life would soon change.

੨▲

CHAPTER TWO

Too Young a Bride

❧

One afternoon when I was twelve and a half years old, I was playing the bone game with my sister and brother in the yard. Suddenly the door opened, and I was happy to see Nicola arriving home so early. He came directly to me, kissed my cheek and said, "Congratulations." My mother came out, smiling. I asked the reason for this, and he told me I was to be engaged to Yeprem that same afternoon. I was stunned. My mother kissed me, and she wished me all the best. My younger sister and brother stopped their game and did the same. I was in shock. I did not even know what "engaged" meant, exactly, or what was expected from me now. I only knew Yeprem by name. The entire city knew him and his family. They were famous for their wealth, their knowledge and their good name. They always helped everyone, Christian or Muslim. It was known in the city that when their grandfather died, the three sons divided the gold coins that were their heritage with a big measuring cup. The older brother had taken two full cups each time for each cup that he gave to his younger brothers. When Yeprem's father had asked him the reason, he answered that he was the first born and this was the custom. The two brothers had each received many cups of large gold coins. They were still working together, and they always respected the older brother. I had heard that Yeprem was a handsome boy. He was at least twenty-four years old, twice my age. My mother felt my pain and surprise. She hugged and kissed me. " Arousiak, you are so lucky!" she said. "All the parents of this city and the neighboring towns wish Yeprem would ask their daughter's hand in marriage. You are entering a palace and you are going to live with a wonderful family. His father and mother are the kindest people in this world, and you will be happy with them. He is their only child. They will treat you like their own daughter. Don't be afraid. All will be good. You will not have to work hard. They have a lot of servants. It will help Nicola, for he will have one less person to worry about."

This last sentence gave me courage. I always felt guilty Nicola had to work so hard to feed and clothe us. Now at least I had the opportunity to do something for my family. Anyway, I did not have much choice either. All the promises had already been made, and in those days this was the way of life for all girls. Deep in my heart I was frightened of the unknown. After all, I was still a child of twelve.

Some days passed, and we received word that the family was going to visit us to arrange the official engagement and decide on the wedding date. Some of our close relatives came to our house to prepare for the festivity. On that special date, they took me to a room and dressed me in a traditional Armenian dress. They added a pretty hair-band decorated with coins, covering my forehead. From behind the curtain I could see musicians holding traditional Armenian musical instruments. With *dhol, tar and ghaval*,[5] they were playing the traditional party music. Behind the musicians were many men holding large brass trays on their heads, with lots of gifts covered with colorful flowers. I saw that there was a tall, strong man behind the musicians, surrounded by an older man and woman. A lot of family members and friends were following behind them. Curious neighbors were also outside watching this ceremony. I understood that the tall man was my future husband, Yeprem. I had mixed feelings. From a distance, he looked attractive. He seemed much bigger than my brother Nicola. I still did not know what I had to do or say. I waited in my room. The music was playing loudly. My brain was empty and I was numb, trying to keep myself busy by playing with the two long braids that were hanging on each side of my shoulders. Suddenly the music became louder, the door opened and my mother entered, smiling. The other women were behind her. They checked to see that my costume was nicely arranged and took me to the living room. The women and men were dancing in front of me, and the women were throwing candies at my feet. I could hear everyone admiring me, saying how beautiful I had become, how lucky Yeprem and I were to belong to each other, that I really looked like the morning star. Many compliments! We all arrived in the living room. The priest was standing in the middle of the room and everyone surrounded him, like a half moon. I was not looking up; my head was down and I felt feverish.

At this moment, the young man approached me and we

[5]-A kind of drum, string instrument like sitar and clarinet.

both stood in front of the priest, who had a beautiful large golden cross in his hand. His assistant was shaking a silver pot, covering us with the sweet smell of the incense *khoung*. The priest blessed us, and the two rings that our *kavor*, the best man and witness, was holding. The *kavor* plays an important role in the newlywed family. After the prayers, the priest asked us to kiss the cross. Yeprem took a ring, which had a large, shiny stone, and put it on my finger. The ring was so heavy and too large for my finger I did not know how to keep it on my finger. Yeprem told me gently, I should not worry, and as he would have it fixed tomorrow. This was the first sentence that I heard from him. He had a very soft and kind voice. He looked so appealing that all my fears suddenly disappeared. At this moment the music started playing, and his mother and father approached me. After kissing me, they said they always had wished to have a daughter, and now God had granted their wishes. Then they put a beautiful necklace on my neck, and Yeprem's father gave me a beautiful bracelet. The stones were glittering in many colors. In the middle there was a beautiful green stone that I learned was an emerald. I had never seen such colorful jewels in my life. My mother and Nicola kissed me. They looked happy and proud. My younger sister and brother were running around, eating and playing. They looked happy, too. I felt I had grown up suddenly. Now I belonged to this older group more than to the little children. But I was still only twelve and a half years old.

Everyone was dancing Armenian dances around us. They asked Yeprem and me to dance. I used to dance nicely. There is a lot of finger and hand movement in Armenian dances. People used to say I had beautiful long fingers, and therefore

20

I was a better dancer. That night, I might have spoken only two words with my future husband. Later we started eating the delicious rice, lamb, *dolma*, and all the food my mother and our relatives had prepared. The music was playing continuously. People were dancing and drinking toasts to our health and happiness. Each time they would make a *kenaz*,[6] someone who had a nice voice would sing in that person's honor. They remembered my father, and we all felt his empty place. But we hoped he was present with us as he had promised Nicola.

After dinner, they removed the flowers from the brass trays, and every one was amazed at the generosity of this family. There were all kinds of gifts: gowns, jewelry, silver dishes, exotic foods, even clothing for my mother, Nicola, Kharse, my sister and brother. They gave us a framed picture of Yeprem as a child standing between his father and my father. It brought tears to our eyes but reminded me that my father would have liked to see us united with this family. After all these emotions, our immediate families gathered seriously for awhile. They decided on the date of the wedding, which was going to be soon, before the end of spring.

Later that night everyone left. But our aunts and grandparents stayed in our house. We were all very tired. My mother and our relatives cleaned the house as much as they could, and they all admired the trays again, looking at my jewelry and gifts. They were repeating over and over again how lucky I was to enter such a good family. Some of my cousins took the rings and necklaces and tried them on in front of the mirror. I still had the red marble and the stone Nicola had given

---

5- Toast.

21

to me so long ago hidden in my pocket, and I was squeezing them with my fingers. I was feeling the warmth of Yeprem around me. I was feeling protected. I had found a husband, a father and a brother all at the same time. His few words made me comfortable. I was no longer afraid of my future.

Since my engagement, our house had not returned to normal. People were visiting us all the time. Our close relatives were helping my mother with all the preparations for the wedding. They were sewing, cooking and doing other chores. They never allowed me to help them with any of the work. Everyone would tell me to go out and play and enjoy the days that were left for me in my father's house. My younger sister and brother no longer played with me; I had become a stranger to them. Nicola was very busy helping my mother. My ring was altered the next day, as Yeprem had promised, and it was back on my finger. I liked to look at it, as it would reflect rainbow colors under the sun. I still continued climbing up the tallest tree. However, this time I was not looking outside but inside. I was remembering my short twelve-and-a-half years living in this house. I remembered my father's face, my mother's sweet smile, such a hardworking couple with no complaints. Mother was never tired and always present for us. I was asking myself, How I could ever do what she was doing? But when I remembered that she, too, had married at a very young age and with a less fortunate man than my future husband, I became more confident. They told me I was about to enter a real castle, with maids and gardeners. But still my mind was tormented. What was I supposed to do as a wife? Deep in my heart I had liked Yeprem, and I was sure all would work out well. From the top of the tree, I looked at the corner of the garden where I had played my last bone game and where it was announced that I had been engaged to Yeprem. This was the moment my childhood had ended. I reviewed my life many times before the wedding, and I sort of threw my childhood away and entered the circle of adulthood.

The wedding date was approaching. Our house was always crowded. The women were busy helping my mother with my dowry, although Yeprem's family had mentioned that we did not need to give them anything. Before the wedding, we were invited to my future home for lunch, but they kept us for dinner, too. Khoy was divided into many sections. Each section was called a *Tagh* and given a name. My parents lived in Post *Tagh*. But Yeprem lived in Aghai *Tagh*. They had a large and a beautiful house. It was in the best neighborhood in the city. For the first time, I saw my mother sitting like a princess with others serving her. She looked serene. I could see on her face that she was really happy for the first time since the death of my father. They had prepared an elaborate meal. They asked Yeprem to show me the garden. It was so large that I was not able to see the end of it. The trees, too, were large and old. The first thing I did was to ask Yeprem if these trees were too big for me to climb on, especially the one tree that stood in front of the house. He told me there was a big nest on the top of that tree and that every year a couple of storks flew into town and lived in that nest until the end of summer. And when the weather got colder, they would fly away until the following year. He said I would enjoy their presence and find the leftover food that the birds throw from their nest each day on the ground around the tree, sometimes the head of a snake, sometimes a lizard or another small animal. He promised I would be able to see the little ones fly with their parents, and at the end of the summer we could watch their departure. I was fascinated with this tree. It was so big I thought a person could live on it. Then he showed me his beautiful white horse. When he introduced me to the horse, the intelligent animal looked at me, shook his head and licked my hands. Birds were singing everywhere in the garden, and the water in the large pond looked so pure that it was almost inviting me to jump in. All around the pond were colorful roses and their fragrance was overwhelming. Butterflies and bees flew all over the garden. Then Yeprem told me a very colorful snake was living in the basement. It never hurt anyone, and tradition said it was the keeper of the house. He said they put some milk in a dish by the basement door every day and the snake would drink it. He said if I saw the snake, I would like it and see that it was harmless. After dinner we returned to our home. Everybody was very happy and my family was talking about the beautiful house and the kindness of our hosts. I was even more reassured, and happy, too. I had a pleasant day. Yeprem had promised he would help me climb the trees and teach me to ride horses. He also told me he would take me on some business trips.

Our wedding day approached quickly. The women took me to the public bath. We bathed with all the other women in a large room clouded with steam. A large pool of cold water sat in the middle. I did not care what the other women were doing. I was determined to cool my body with the fresh water, and I was lost deep in my thoughts. At noon we returned home. After drinking tea and eating sweets, the special ceremony began. They put *Henna* on my fingers and toes, and then everyone started to dress up and prepare for the wedding. I was left alone for a moment. They suggested I take a nap and relax as I was going to have a long night. I lay down on my bed. The steam and the noise had tired me. I closed my eyes and fell asleep.

I do not know how many hours passed, but when I opened my eyes I saw my room filled with women. They were dressed beautifully. Some were singing, some talking loudly. They were eager to dress me up. A long dress was hanging in my room, a traditional Armenian dress with a *kotik* [7]. I jumped out of bed. They made me sit in a chair, and the makeup lady started to groom my eyebrows. It was painful but did not take long. Everyone agreed I looked much nicer. She drew lines around my eyes with *kohl* [8] and put color on my lips. I started to look more like a woman than a girl of my age. After they dressed me up, my mother, as always, combed my long golden-brown hair gently and slowly, as if she were registering it in her memory for as long as she could. She looked happy. But at the same time I could see sadness deep in her eyes. She put the *kotik* on my head and I could feel the cold touch of the coins on my skin. I was admiring myself. They kept me in front of the mirror so that I felt glamorous for the first time. I saw a little girl who had a woman's face. A girl, who should have been at school, but was about to get married.

Soon we heard all the noises outside. There was loud music mingled with the cries of children and adults. They told me to stay in my room while everyone went out. I looked out of my window from behind the curtain. I recog-

[7]- Hair band.
[8]- Black powder used as eyeliner.

nized Yeprem. His mother and father surrounded him, and they had a lot of guests around them. Again there were many trays full of gifts. On the first tray I could see my white wedding gown. Yeprem looked so strong and handsome I couldn't take my eyes away from him. They entered our house. For a moment there was silence, and then I heard the traditional wedding music approaching my room. When the door opened, I saw Yeprem surrounded by men and women. Nicola and my mother came in first, kissed me and put my hands in the hands of Yeprem. I could see tears in my mother's eyes. She begged him to be nice to me and build a strong family. Yeprem kissed my mother's hand and thanked her for giving him such a precious flower and reassured her that he would always be gentle with me, that she should not worry.

We walked side by side to the living room where everyone was waiting for us. As soon as we entered the room, everyone present threw candies and coins at us. Yeprem took me to his parents. They kissed me and said some kind words. Then, with the *kavor*, we walked to the table with the tray that held my wedding dress. The priest and his assistants were waiting for us. The music and the talking stopped. All was silent, and the priest started the prayers. He blessed us, and then he blessed my wedding dress. Again coins and candies were thrown at us. My younger sister and brother and all the other children in the room were running to collect the coins and candies. But I was standing still. I was not a child anymore. Soon I was going to be called Mrs. Yepremi Hayrapetian. What a responsibility!

After picking up the large tray, the women took me to my room. They took off the dress that I was wearing, and I was dressed from head to toe in a beautiful white wedding dress.

Everything I wore was white with silk and lace that had been woven by a woman from our city who was famous for her handiwork. It was a very beautiful dress. There were stones and pearls embroidered on it. My underwear, shoes, and even stockings were trimmed with lace. Then my mother put a new white satin *kotik* on my head, this time covered with real gold coins. I believe they had been working on my wedding dress since our engagement. I looked like an angel, white and shining. The only childish look was my long braids, but this was a traditional Armenian hairdo. When I was ready, Yeprem came to take me to the church. Now it was serious! I was going to leave my own home forever. There is a song that is played at every wedding: "They are taking her away, they are separating her from us." I do not know why they sing this song, because when they do, everyone, especially the mothers and brides always cry. Maybe the musicians give them a reason to pour out their sadness officially.

After the ceremony we walked out and left for church. Now, I was accompanied by Yeprem and our *kavor*. The rest of the family and guests were following. We did not talk much. But sometimes we looked timidly at each other and our eyes would meet. He was holding my cold hand with his large warm hand. I felt secure with his strength. Our wedding bands were shining and my diamond ring was twinkling like a star. I remembered my mother had asked me not to be afraid, to accept bravely what Yeprem would ask me to do that night. She told me the honor of our family depended on the first night of our wedding. Handing me a white handkerchief, she said Yeprem knew what he had to do and that I should be obedient and a good wife. She said that after a little pain all would go well. She had confidence in me, and she knew that I would always honor my family.

I was not sure what all this meant. But since my engagement, my mother had kept me in the company of her friends. Once in awhile, one of the more daring women would speak out boldly to give me information about womanhood. Sometimes I was too embarrassed to listen, but I was also curious to learn what adulthood was all about and what the difference was between a girl and a woman. Now I was close to crossing this line.

Entering the church, we walked directly to the altar where the priest was waiting. Our town church was one of the largest of all the surrounding cities. People from other villages would come here for important events. There were many gold and silver crosses, beautiful paintings of Jesus and Mary, and as in all the Armenian churches, a painting of *Sourp Mesrop Mashtoz*, the founder of our alphabet. In each painting he is represented with a tablet in his hands and the Armenian letters engraved on the tablet. His eyes always look toward the sky where his knowledge had come from. That is why the title Sourp is given to him, as he is a saint to us.

The altar was decorated with hundreds of colorful roses. The perfume of the roses was mixed with the traditional smell of the incense, which was filling the air. When our *kavor*, Yeprem and I stood in front of the priest, he started his prayers. At the end of his readings he asked us if in health or sickness, happiness or sadness and any other occasions of our life we would love and cherish each other and promise to build a traditional Armenian home filled with children. We both said "yes," and we exchanged our wedding bands for a second time. But this time the rings were taken from our right hand and put on our left hand to show that we were married now. The priest called us Mr. and Mrs. Yepremi Hayrapetian, and he asked Yeprem to kiss his bride. He kissed me timidly on my cheek. I felt his warm lips on me and I trembled. When we turned toward our families he stepped on my foot very gently. This was a tradition to show everyone that he was going to be the boss. Everyone laughed as we kissed the golden cross and walked to our families. They kissed us and blessed us. Both mothers had tears of joy - and sadness in their eyes. I was holding back my tears and walking straight ahead, not looking back. My mother had said that I had to behave appropriately. We all hugged and kissed each other. Candies and coins were covering us. I had never seen so many candies in my whole life.

We all went to Yeprem's house. At the entrance door there was a large glass plate on the floor, and, as was the tradition, my husband and I walked on it and broke the plate. This was the sign of good luck for newlyweds entering their new home. Many people were invited to our wedding. There were twenty or more servers bringing food and drinks to the tables. The house and the garden were decorated like a fairy tale. I could not believe my eyes. It was like a dream. The garden looked like Paradise. As soon as we entered the house, his mother and father offered me more bracelets and necklaces, much more elegant than my engagement gifts. I was asking myself what I could do with all this jewelry. They guided us to the main table that was very big. Yeprem and I and the rest of our family sat at the head and the guests sat around us. They started toasting and singing. They toasted my father, our ancestors, and even our country of Armenia. Everyone looked happy, enjoying the delicious food and charming music. We all danced the traditional dances and had a wonderful time. Even my brother and sister did not look sleepy. They were running around and laughing. They had made new friends with children from Yeprem's family.

I was given a cup of wine, and I sipped slowly. I was feeling relaxed and kind of out of this world. The music, the decorations and the scent of flowers had taken away all my fear. I loved Yeprem, I was attracted to him, and I was feeling nobody could hurt me anymore. I was lucky to be his wife. Still, a small inner voice was crying for my lost childhood, my lost dreams of education and knowledge of reading and writing.

Much past midnight, the elderly guests said that they had to let the bride and groom rest. We stood up, and the music accompanied Yeprem and me to our bedroom. When we entered the room, we heard the guests begin to leave. As soon as we were alone, I pulled the handkerchief from my pocket and handed it to Yeprem. I said my mother had asked me to give it to him. He took it from me with apparent discomfort and put it on the bedside table. I did not know what to do. For the first time, I was alone in a room in the presence of the man who was called my husband. He took off my hairband and said it must have been heavy. Handing me a glass of sweet wine, he said, "Let's drink to our new life. Do not worry. I love you and I will take care of you. You will always be my queen and I will protect you. I hope God has put an easy road in front of us, too."

As I was drinking the wine, I looked at my husband. He had taken off his jacket and looked very attractive. I had never seen him at such close range. With each drop of wine entering my body, I knew I would be happy with him, that I could trust and love him forever, as the priest had said, in good times and bad times.

Yeprem approached me and said I must be tired by now and that I should rest. He opened the buttons of my dress gently, while he was caressing me softly. I was feeling warm and lost. I could feel my heart beating hard. I was pulled toward him. Everything went very fast, and we became, officially, husband and wife. While I was still lying on the bed covered with a white shiny quilted blanket, Yeprem put on his robe, opened the door and handed the bloody handkerchief to his mother. Then he came back to me, kissed my cheek, and we both fell into a deep sleep.

When I woke up the next morning, sunshine was bathing our beautiful room. I looked around and saw that each piece of furniture was in exquisite taste. It looked like a room in a palace. My husband also opened his eyes. He told me he had been awake for awhile but he was watching me sleep and did not want to wake me up. As we dressed, he asked me how I felt. My mother and father-in-law were sitting in the garden. We approached them, and they kissed us and guided us to the table under the old tree where an elaborate breakfast was waiting for us. They gave us the traditional liquid *halvah*, which is called *hassoudah*, made from flour, oil and sugar. This food usually is for newlyweds and women after the birth of a child. They say it strengthens the body. Yeprem said the storks were going to arrive very soon. We went for a walk in the garden. I smelled the flowers and we listened to the songs of the birds. In the distance, we could see the mountains. We were in the same city where I had grown up, but everything was so different and beautiful that I thought this house was in another country. At noon, my mother, Nicola, his wife and my sister and brother arrived. My mother-in-law had invited them for lunch in order to please. But even as we kissed each other, it now seemed very natural for me to be living away from my mother. After lunch, we opened more gifts that had continued to arrive. There were all kinds of beautiful objects. When my mother was leaving, she told me, "You see, I told you that you have entered into a dream palace. Thank you for keeping the honor of our family. I hope God will protect you both."

The days passed, one after the other, smoothly and sweetly. I did not have much to do. I would walk in the garden, smell the roses, admire nature and talk to my in-laws and spend pleasant moments with my husband. Soon he taught me to climb the tall trees that had seemed impossible for me. When he taught me to ride his beautiful horse, it was my most enjoyable time. Such a friendly, intelligent horse. Later, he bought me a horse of my own so that we could ride together, side by side. One day I saw the colorful snake that was protecting our house. Every day I would fill a dish with fresh milk for the snake. Sometimes we could see the mark of his body traced on the sand in the basement, where he had made a hole to live in. One afternoon while we were having tea under the old tree, Yeprem told me to look up. Suddenly I saw two large, black and white beautiful birds approaching the tree. It was breathtaking. Their heads were tilted down as if they were greeting us. It was amazing to see these birds coming directly to their old nest. How did they remember where it was? They had been away for almost eight months, and Yeprem told me they had come from a long distance. God has given every creature amazing intelligence and intuition.

32

Yeprem went to work every day with his father, and sometimes they came home for lunch. My life was peaceful. Sometimes my mother-in-law and I would visit my mother. We would always bring gifts for her. They were all doing well, and my mother looked much happier. Five months after our wedding, I woke up one morning and I saw that I was bleeding. My bed was stained with blood, and I was scared to death, thinking maybe I had a fatal disease and that I was going to die. I started crying and that woke up Yeprem. When he learned what had happened, he hugged me and said not to worry, that now I had become a real woman. He called his mother, and she gave me some clean cloths and taught me what to do. This happened near my thirteenth birthday.

My mother-in-law was really like a second mother to me. She was such a loving and caring person. She always tried to make life comfortable and easy for me. She did not have much to do around the house since the servants did all the work. Sometimes we would dress up and visit relatives who were less fortunate, taking along gifts and food. She would always say, "You have to appreciate what God has given to you and share it with others." Occasionally we would go to church, and at other times she would sew or weave laces, teaching me her skills. She would say that it is always good to master some kind of art or craft in life. She knew a lot about herbs and curing illnesses. When we would go in the garden, picking leaves and flowers, she would teach me about the healing quality of each one. When a maid was ill, she would often be able to cure her in a day with the help of these herbs. Or she would give her a special massage and the pain would disappear. She taught me all her secrets. Many people had heard about her, and whenever neighbors were ill, they would come to her. I learned quickly how to help her.

The other interesting activity in our house was our weekly bread-baking day. An Armenian woman, Banafsheh, who had lost her husband some years before, was the breadmaker of the village. Banafsheh had four children to take care of. Nasik, her older daughter, was my age. But she was much smaller and more fragile than I. She was always attached to the skirt of her mother. They would come to our house for two days, but sometimes my mother-in-law would keep them a day longer so they could be fed and rested before leaving. Banafsheh was a very hard-working woman, going from house to house to bake bread. The first day she would knead the dough and let it rise all night. Very early the next morning, she would warm up the oven, which actually was a large hole dug in the ground especially for this purpose. All the inside walls of the oven were covered smoothly with clay, and there was a place to burn wood for heat. When the oven was not in use, it was covered, to protect and keep it clean. Banafsheh used a large, round, flat piece of wood, which was padded and covered with white cotton. This was the mold for the bread. She would knead the dough on a table. When it was nice and round, she would put it on the mold and hit it against the wall of the oven. The dough would stick to the side of the wall. Later, when the bread was baked, she would pull it out with the help of a large flat wooden spatula. In the morning when we would wake up, the pile of bread was almost as high as the top of my head. This bread is called *lavash* [9]. The servants would put these freshly baked breads

---

[9]- It is baked to this day and can be found in many stores. But it is not as big and fresh as the kind we used to enjoy.

in clean white linen towels and store them in the basement on a special shelf. Under these shelves there was a deep drawer. Yeprem and my father-in-law used to keep their guns and ammunitions hidden in the depth of this drawer, and they would cover them with large wooden boards looking like shelves, then they would put many layers of bread on the top of it.

No one was aware of this hidden drawer. I did not learn about it until much later. The first two days the bread would stay soft. Later, though, it became dry. So when we wanted to eat it, they would spray a little water, cover it for a short time, and again the bread would turn soft and edible. I was always happy when the bread baking day came because Nasik and I had become close friends. She would accompany her mother everywhere. She was lonely since she did not have many friends. In a way, I needed a friend of my own age, too. She always respected me as her mistress but for me there was no difference between us. We would go into the garden, far from everyone, and become two young girls, playing the bone game, jumping rope. Sometimes I would give her some of my dresses, and once I asked Yeprem's permission to give her a piece of my jewelry. At first, Nasik refused it. But when I insisted, her eyes shone with joy at owning a small ring for her finger. My mother-in-law was pleased, too. And I learned to give more to people in need. For the New Year, we gave a gleaming golden necklace to my mother. She was so pleased and proud that she wore it all the time.

My life with Yeprem could not have been better. People were right to say that I was lucky to enter into such a loving family. All was going well with us. We spent our time together walking, playing cards, riding horses, climbing trees, watching the birds and loving each other more and more every day. The storks had now repaired their nests, and I could see one sitting on the nest while the other one would hunt for food. Yeprem had said I could find all kinds of left-over food on the ground around the tree. This was the sign that they already had their little ones. One day we saw four of them flying away and coming back to their nest. Yeprem told me that the parents were teaching their little ones to fly.

When summer ended, one day we saw four large black and white birds flying around our house and the tree as if they were telling us goodbye. They flew high and far away. We followed them with our eyes as much as we could until they disappeared in the clouds. My heart felt pain. Yeprem held me in his arms and told me the months would fly fast and I would see them coming back to their nest the following year.

Just two events made me sad for a day. Most mornings, about eleven-thirty, I would go to my room, close the door and watch the children from behind the curtain. They were coming home from school at that time, and this was the only moment of my day I would feel sad. Although I had a good life, school was still my fondest dream. My mother-in-law knew about my pain and my secret, but she did not say anything to me. She was trying to teach me her knowledge of natural medicine so that it would satisfy my yearning for education. One day while I was hiding behind the heavy curtain watching the boys coming home for lunch, Yeprem arrived home early. He came in the room looking for me. When he saw me behind the curtain, he asked what I was doing. I answered that I was watching the boys coming back from school. He urged me to pull back the curtain and never do it again. Suddenly I rebelled. I said he could not stop me. If I wanted to, I would continue to watch. He came closer, looked at me seriously and gave me a little tap on my cheek. I was shocked, and for a second, I was scared. Gently, he said that he was the man of the house. When he said something, I should obey and not argue. This was the only such incident in our whole life together. Later he tried to make me forget this event. He told me he would teach me how to write better and would bring me some books in the future. He explained how the country was structured. If it were different, he would have sent me to school, too.

The second event happened one night when Yeprem and I were playing cards. Most nights he would give me coins and we would play cards with money. Each of us had our little capital to play the game. One night we played very long and I started losing all my coins. I asked to continue on credit. He accepted but I was still losing. I was hoping that I would win and pay him back. But it never happened. Finally he wanted to stop the game but he wanted his money. He had such a serious face that I answered, timidly, that I did not have any money to pay my debts. He told me he would accept anything from my own belongings. I went to our room and saw my wedding dress. That was the only thing I thought belonged to me. I took it gently in my arms and held it close to my heart. Little tears filled my eyes. When I came down the stairs, my tears started dropping faster. As I approached Yeprem, I handed him my gown and started crying wildly. "This is all that I have to pay you with," I said, and continued crying. It seemed that life had ended for me. He started laughing. He took me in his arms, kissed me and said he was teasing. He did not expect that I would believe him, and added that all he owned also belonged to me.

There was only one activity in our house that never belonged to me, and actually it was even strictly prohibited to me. Every week the Armenian *Fedaees* [10] would come to our house for meetings, but I was not allowed to participate. I could hear in the conversations between my husband and his father that the world outside was not as peaceful as our house. They were talking about dangerous conditions in Europe, and it had been awhile since they had last traveled. But for me all these places were so far away that I was not concerned. We had our secure life. That was enough. But more and more, people were coming to our house for social and political meetings, and Yeprem was taking part in them.

Yeprem was the head of the Armenian school in town. Since he knew many Persian authorities, and had finished his studies, he was the main liaison between Persians and the church to keep the Armenian schools open in order to teach our religion and language with the standard Persian curriculum to the Armenian students. He was also active in the political group, *Dashnak*[10], in our village. He always said that we had to keep our Armenian schools, churches and the Armenian population of the villages safe from all outside danger. The men would come by night and they would leave our house, one by one, before daylight, in order not to attract any attention. After all, we were surrounded by Muslims and Turks, who had long been the enemies of Armenia. We had a secret basement in our house. The secret door was in the living room and a big colorful Persian rug was hiding it. At night when all the servants were in their

---

[10]- Activists.

rooms, Yeprem would open the door and tell me to go to our room. When it was time to feed the group, he would tap on the wall. It meant that my mother-in-law would take them some food. There was a large table in the basement and we would prepare the samovar in advance. In winter we had to heat the place, as the winters were very cold and the guests usually stayed there for hours. When Yeprem would tap on the wall, I was not supposed to leave my room. But sometimes I helped my mother-in-law, and I would take food to the secret door out of curiosity. Yeprem would come to the door to take the tray from us. He would tell us to return to our beds and go to sleep. The nights he held the meetings, he would come to bed very late. I was not supposed to ask questions about these people or their meetings.

When I was fourteen, almost a year and half after our wedding, I woke up nauseated one morning. I did not feel that I could put anything into my mouth and that if I drank the morning milk I would vomit. I tried to pretend that all was going well with me. But my mother-in-law was the first to remark on the changes. She asked the reason for my indisposition. I explained how I was feeling. She asked me if I had been bleeding lately. I replied that I was happy that I had not had a period for a long time. She screamed loudly and called her husband and son who were leaving for their office. I was surprised, as I had never heard her talking in such a loud voice. When they came in, she kissed me and said to Yeprem that soon we would be parents. She thanked God and us for making them grandparents.

Our joy was complete. Everyone was happy about my pregnancy. Soon we all started preparing garments for the baby. For me it was as if we were going to buy a big doll. We started decorating the baby's room. After some months, everyone could see I was expecting a baby. I was feeling better, but I could no longer ride the horse or climb trees. Everyone was looking after me.

Months passed. I could feel the baby inside my body, kicking the walls of my abdomen. It was a joy for all of us to know that a new member would be added to our family. Soon the nine months had passed, and finally the labor started. Yeprem had hired the best midwife in the city. When my pain became sharper, she came and took me to my bedroom. My mother and mother-in-law were holding my hands. They put cool cloths over my forehead and mouth, encouraging me to be brave, to push and help finish the birth fast so that my suffering would end sooner. I was very calm, ignoring the fears and pain. I knew this would soon be over, so I was able to do what they asked. After some time, I felt release, and I heard a baby cry for the first time. They said, "It is a beautiful girl." I almost fainted from the hard labor and stress. When I came back to my senses, they showed me my daughter and I called her Liana. I had fallen in love with this name several months ago. We had guests from Armenia, cousins of my mother-in-law. They had a beautiful daughter whose name was Liana. They said this was the name of a beautiful valley in Armenia, covered with red poppies, and blue and yellow flowers. I loved the little girl and her name. When Yeprem came to see the baby and me, I asked him to call her Liana. But he said that we could not do so, as we had to name her after his deceased grandmother, Lousik. But he promised that our next girl would be called Liana.

As soon as I got back my strength, we had a big party in our house and many people came for this occasion. The priest baptized Lousik. Now she was officially a Christian. It was a nice ceremony. When the priest immersed her in water, she smiled and her godfather hung a little golden cross around her neck. It is a tradition with Armenians to baptize the baby after its birth. They say if something happens to the baby after he is baptized, he will go directly to Heaven.

After several months she started teething, and this was the occasion for another festivity, *adam hadik* [11].

Lousik grew to be a lovely little girl. She had my golden-brown hair and her father's deep black eyes. She had started walking and running, pronouncing some words. I was hoping her destiny would not be like mine, that she would be able to go to school and study like the European girls Kharse had told me about.

&

[11]. We prepare a dish with wheat and beans; we add raisins, walnuts and candies to it. We hold a white cloth over the baby's head and someone drops a little of this adam hadik on the cloth. They put different instruments around the baby, representing different types of professions. As soon as the baby picks up one of the instruments, they interpret it to be his future profession. If the baby picks up a pair of scissors, they say that the baby will become a barber or a tailor. Then everyone eats some adam hadik and takes some home.

CHAPTER THREE

A Trip Abroad

∂♠

By the time Lousik was almost two-and-a-half years old, the First World War broke out in Europe. One day Yeprem and his father talked seriously for awhile. We did not know what they were saying. But in the morning Yeprem prepared his horses and the large wagon we owned. He and his father gathered some belongings and coins, and he told my mother-in-law and me we were going to Armenia. He had to take care of some business and also had some orders to participate in meetings. I was both happy and shocked. It was incomprehensible to me. Why were we going on such a trip when I was pregnant for a second time and approaching the end of my pregnancy? They had always told me not to ride horses. But as my in-laws were travelling with us, I was more comforted. We went to visit my family. Nicola and Yeprem talked for awhile, and we left the city for the first time. Yeprem and his parents were very attentive to our daughter and me. But he was pensive and withdrawn. We stopped in many cities and villages and spent the nights in safe caravansaries[12]. It was an interesting trip but I was not in a con-

---

12. Inns.

dition to enjoy it. When we arrived in Armenia, we stayed with our relatives who had visited us in Khoy with their daughter Liana. I was getting heavy and tired. My mother-in-law was taking good care of me.

The first thing we saw in our ancestors' land was Mount Ararat with its snowy top, and I was trying to imagine how Noah with his ark had ended up on the top of this mountain. I remembered stories of my father and brother, and I felt closer to my father. Lousik started playing with her new friends. She was an active and loving child. She also was the only person who could bring a smile to Yeprem's pensive face. Yeprem was worrying about my approaching childbirth, but they had already hired a woman to assist me during the labor. One morning I found Lousik red and burning with fever. My mother-in-law and I immediately did all that we could. Nothing helped. She was becoming weaker, and she refused to drink or eat any food. Yeprem immediately went to find a doctor. When he returned with the doctor, he asked him to do all that he could to help the baby. He told him that money was no object. If needed, he would travel to Russia even though they were engaged in a horrible war, and bring any needed medication. We were approaching the end of May 1915. The doctor did all he could, but there was no improvement in my child's condition. Her little body was covered with red spots. They called her sickness the measles. She had an infection in her little chest and was coughing badly. I was not able to move fast as I was weighed down by my pregnancy. I was sitting by her bedside, holding her little burning hands. While I was changing the wet cloths on her forehead, I repeated the prayers that I learned from my mother. My tears were falling like a river. Sometimes I felt as if there were no more tears left in my eyes.

Yeprem was worried, but he was trying to stay strong. My mother-in-law used all her knowledge of medicine, but nothing helped. One morning when I was trying to call Lousik to open up her beautiful eyes to make her drink a little water, I suddenly saw my father's face smiling at me through my tears. It was Lousik that I was looking at, but it was my father I was seeing. When I took her hands in my hand, they felt cold and motionless. I remembered how Nicola had described our father's high fever and his death, and I fainted. When I opened my eyes everyone was present in the room, crying over the little body of our daughter. My in-laws were heartbroken and crying quietly. I saw tears falling from Yerpem's eyes for the first time. His face was wet and his eyes were lost in the distance.

I kissed my daughter's cold face. Everyone told me she had become a little angel. I asked myself, Why did she come into this world? Could she not become an angel in the other world? What did God want from us? Were we His baby-sitters? I had been so happy for all these years, why could this not continue forever? Did they not say in the fairy tales that the prince and princess lived happily ever after? Why not us? I was crying, and at the same time I was feeling another new life kicking me gently, reminding me of its existence. I really did not want to have that baby born now. What was the use? Was this baby also destined to die?

We prepared a burial for Lousik. Yeprem found the best plot in the cemetery. He bought a pretty little box for her eternal house. The most important priest pronounced the prayers. How could a person bury a beautiful little being in the cold ground without protection? We were crying, that was all we were able to do. None of the biblical words pronounced by the priest comforted us. Even the priest was not sure how to justify this unjustifiable act. There was no reason for such a tragedy, even though we were aware that at that same moment hundreds of young soldiers were dying for their country in Europe. On the contrary, now my knowledge had grown and I could feel all the pain of the mothers who had lost their children.

We stayed at home, surrounded by our extended family and friends. We prayed and cried. I was feeling more and more uncomfortable. The pain of labor was getting intense. But I had made up my mind not to bear another miserable human being into this world. I was keeping all the pain to myself, trying, instead, to postpone this labor and to comfort Yeprem. It was the first of June, a month after the Ascension. I was thinking of my house in our town, of my mother. I was in my ancestors' land, a stranger, sad and confused. Yeprem and I were blaming ourselves for the death of our daughter, but not aloud to each other. On the first of June, we all went to the cemetery for the seventh day after the death of our daughter. The priest prayed over her little tomb. We burned incense and we covered the grave with fresh cut flowers.

Many people came to our house with tears and comforting words. They asked us to sit at the table for lunch so everyone could sit down and rest, too. As soon as I sat down, I felt a sharp pain. Although I was trying to postpone the birth of my baby, *I felt that the force of nature was much stronger*. The midwife whom we had contacted for the labor was present at the luncheon. Yeprem noted my discomfort, alerted her, and with the help of my mother-in-law, they carried me to another room.

This was much different from the last time. Everything went much faster. Suddenly I heard the cry of the baby, and I recognized a voice that was like Lousik's. They announced that it was a beautiful girl. After awhile Yeprem came in wearing a smile through his tears. He took the baby in his arms and he told me that Liana was born to bring us happiness. Our happiness was both sweet and sour. One child was dead and another one was born, all within one week.

We had to stay in Armenia until Yeprem could finish his business. I was breastfeeding the baby, comparing her constantly with Lousik. Soon Liana became her own person and Lousik became like a dream. I was happy to have Liana but inside of me there was an open wound. I tried not to touch this wound and to live with what was given to us. I never visited Lousik's grave after the seventh day of the burial, because in our tradition mothers who have borne new babies are not allowed to visit cemeteries.

One day Yeprem received a telegram from our Serpazan Melik Tangian of Tabriz, the highest priest in the state of Azerbaijan. He asked Yeprem to return to Persia immediately. He told him the Turks had left Persia and the authorities were trying to close the existing Armenian schools in the town. He said that Yeprem's presence was needed badly and that the conflicts had calmed down. When Yeprem explained the contents of the telegram to his father, his father suggested that it was too soon to return home. He did not think the political situation was calm yet. But Yeprem decided to return immediately. He said he could not refuse Serpazan Hayr. When we arrived at our home in Khoy, everyone was happy to see us. It was so good to return to our families and our daily life. I had seen the cities and countries that I used to dream about. Now I was happy to be in my own garden, with the people I loved most and felt secure with. No one had learned about the death of Lousik. They cried at her loss, but soon Liana filled their hearts with joy. I was only sixteen years old. I had been married happily for three years, borne two babies, and suffered the loss of one child.

The political situation was not good anywhere. The World War was present on the horizon, although there was no immediate impact on our daily lives. The war seemed far away, but its shadow was present even in the tiny villages. Yeprem was aware of the hidden danger.

Our life was continuing as before, but something had changed. Sometimes in the middle of joy, my tears would fall and sometimes I would see that Yeprem was sad. We were both feeling guilty about Lousik's death. If Yeprem had not been obliged to travel maybe this would not have happened. My mother and mother-in-law both were touched by Lousik's death, and they both helped me in putting it behind. They told me that I should not question death or God's will but that I should be thankful for all His blessings and enjoy Liana. They, too, had lost children, and that is how the world is. They said I should take care of Yeprem and Liana and help others in need.

Liana started sitting, crawling, making noises, teething, walking and then running and pronouncing little words. She had become a beautiful, sweet little girl. Everyone loved her. She really took our minds away from our tragedy and back to normal. Nicola and Kharse's daughter had also turned into a beautiful girl. Both children were adding happiness to our lives.

We continued to go to the yearly picnics with our families.

The Survivor

It was so comforting to see the beautiful green valleys, the snowy top of the mountains and the pure water running across the lands. We would collect wild flowers and herbs for food and medicine. We would also watch and guess the future weddings to come. Once a year, everyone would visit the old church to pray and burn candles. Some would say that it was built in the honor of a *Sourp*[13] named Sarkis and they would also say that Vartan Zoravir, the Armenian hero was buried in this church. I think it was not so important who was where.

But it was important that all the Armenians of the neighboring cities and villages would gather to pray and be together for a day. Yeprem, my in-laws, my mother and others would join us to participate in these ceremonies.

The storks came and left with their new babies. Nasik still came to our house with her mother to bake bread. Her mother filled our house with the sweet smell of fresh bread but the piles were getting higher, as Yeprem had told us to store more bread at home.

We started remodeling our house. We needed to have more comfort for my in-laws, as they were getting older. They were, as always, kind and loving toward me, and to all the people surrounding them. We told the employees to watch the snake's hole and not to harm it. One day I found my mother-in-law very upset. When I asked the reason, she hesitated. But upon my insistence she said that when the maid had gone to the basement to get some bread, she found that the snake had been killed by one of the workers. Although it was just a superstition, we all believed the snake was the guardian of our good fortune, and we were saddened by its loss.

13- Saint.

CHAPTER FOUR

Too Soon a Widow

❧

Yeprem started having more and more meetings in our house. He was preoccupied by the outside political situation. He was not telling us anything. But I was able to overhear when I was serving tea to him and his father as they were talking under the old tree. Both were very pensive. As soon as I approached, they changed the subject. Liana brought them both much joy. She was almost three years old. She loved her father, and whenever Yeprem would come home, minutes before his arrival, Liana was near the door waiting for him and her grandfather. Everyone loved her.

One night when I was taking food to the secret door, I heard one of the men announcing the deportation and killing of many Armenians. I heard the names of the famous *Fedaiis*, Keri and Karo. I learned they were in our house. When Yeprem opened the secret door, the conversation changed and I did not understand if they were talking about present or past history. I did not dare ask Yeprem about this.

I had grown much taller since my marriage, and everyone admired my beauty. My sister was also turning into a pretty girl. She still had several years left to enjoy her life before getting married. She had a comfortable life with my mother, Kharse, and our brothers. Nicola and my younger brother had traveled to Russia, and they stayed there longer since the roads were closed because of the war. We were visiting my mother, my sister-in-law their daughter and my sister more often in my brother's absence, and everyone was doing very well.

One day Yeprem gave me some large bags and asked me to keep all my jewelry in one place. I obeyed immediately. I did not ask the reason. When he said something, I would obey without question. I was not wearing any of the jewelry since the death of Lousik. What was the use of carrying all these precious stones around?

One day Yeprem rushed home very early and he talked with his father for awhile. I heard his father urging Yeprem to leave his parents where they were and to take Liana and me away. Finally Yeprem told me to take necessary clothing for us and for Liana and the bag of jewelry, and he brought another big bag of gold coins. He prepared the white horse and put the bags on it, I kissed my in-laws. Yeprem helped me mount the horse. At that very moment, while he was handing me Liana, a young boy arrived at our door and told Yeprem not to leave. This was an order from the Dashnak party (The Armenian political group that was active to protect the Armenians, the Armenian churches, schools and their country.) Yeprem was told to gather the men of the city and protect their church and families until *General Andranik*[14].

---

[14]. The famous Armenian soldier, arrived in Khoy in order to protect us from the Turkish invasion. Andranik was an Armenian hero who had fought against the Turkish army. He was buried in the Pere-Lachaise Cemetery in Paris, and a large statue, showing him on horseback, was erected on his tomb. Some years ago, the Armenian community moved his remains to Armenia and buried him with all the respect and honor that a hero deserves.

Yeprem, who had Liana in his arms, gave her to my mother-in-law. He helped me down from the horse, took all the bags off the horse and put them back in our room. I did not know why he had wanted to leave, but now all was clear. They were expecting an attack from the Turkish army. The Turks had already massacred many Armenians and destroyed their villages and cities in Turkey and now they were taking advantage of the weakened Persian monarchy and killing us inside the borderlines of Persia. Some Muslim Persians were also eager to help them, as after all we were Christians and they considered us *nagess*, meaning dirty. This was a title given to us during the reign of Shah Abbas, the King of Persia, who had brought a lot of Armenian craftsmen to Persia and settled them mostly in Esfahan, a beautiful city in south of the capital that is famous for its architecture, arts and crafts. As the Armenian girls were pretty and different from the local girls, some men started molesting them, so the Armenians complained to the authorities. In order to protect the girls, the autorities decided to call the Armenians *nagess* so that the men would leave the young girls alone. At that time the *nagess* name was for protection, but now it was turning against us. I was worried about our future. But looking at Yeprem and at his strength, I was sure that he could protect us. Everyone loved him. Who would harm us? And Andranik was on his way to our city. I was content to stay with our family in our house. I was afraid to travel again. Did I not lose Lousik because of our trip? Young men were coming to our house and bringing news to Yeprem and he would leave with them for hours.

We had visited my mother; everyone was awaiting a big storm but no one could see the clouds. When Banafsheh came to our house, she looked very upset. She told us some days ago she heard Andranik was holding a large meeting out of town. She went there with her two sons. Andranik was wearing his traditional uniform and sitting high on his horse so that every one could see him. He talked loudly and invited all the people of the villages to follow him out of there. He said that the Turks were getting ready to attack Khoy and all the surrounding villages. As soon as he left the city Turks would attack and kill every one. She said people asked him if it was not dangerous for him to face the Turks, at that moment he opened his shirt and showed us the cross that was his birth sign. It was a little raised cross from the skin of his chest.

Banafsheh had tears in her eyes. She said that she saw the cross with her own eyes. It was very impressive, as if someone had carved the cross with his skin. Andranik told everyone he was born with this cross. It had always protected him and nobody would be able to kill or harm him. She said some people followed him, but many, like her, had nowhere to go especially those with young children. Some did not even believe him and could not imagine why the Turks would come and kill them? They had been living in these villages for many years and Turks had never killed them.

She said that on the way back home she talked with her sons and everyone agreed that they would stay in Khoy. At least they had a house and jobs here. Where could they go and how would they survive in another city? Now it was clear to me why we had so many meetings lately in the basement and why Yeprem was so pensive and why we were about to leave the other day.

Banafsheh did not stay long in our house. When she was

leaving, she said, "Forgive me if I have said or done something wrong to you. I believe what Andranik told us is true. I am afraid for my children's safety. If I do not see you anymore I want to thank you for everything." We all hugged and kissed each other in tears not knowing if we would see each other again.

Suddenly very late one night, we heard a loud noise. We thought Andranik had arrived. As we approached and Yeprem opened the door, we saw Dr. Eftekhar, a Muslim and Yeprem's best friend, all pale standing at the doorway. He urged Yeprem to take Liana and me and to follow him on his horse. Yeprem did not ask any questions. His father said that he should act very fast and do as he was told. "Do not think about us. We are old, and there is no danger for us. Just go." In haste, he ran upstairs, picked up the two bags containing the gold coins and the jewelry, and we all kissed my mother and father-in-law and followed the doctor on our horse.

It was very dark outside. No one was in the streets. We were not able to see more than a foot in front of us. Our horses, with their intelligence and old habits, were driving us forth. Soon we arrived at the doctor's house. We had been invited to this house many times in the past. It was very large and beautiful, with old trees and a very big garden. None of his servants was at the door. He opened the gate and we saw that one of his wives, who was Armenian, was waiting for us with a lamp in her hand. I felt a little better to see a small light. Liana was sleeping in my arms. We were so hurried and in such shock that we were not even afraid of the future. They helped Liana and me dismount from the horse. They took us to the back of the house, and I realized that they had a hidden basement similar to ours. They told Yeprem to stay inside in the daytime. He was to come out to get air and walk only at night.

Dr. Eftekar told Yeprem he was aware that the Turkish army was present in Khoy, and they knew that Yeprem was the chief of the Armenians in the city and that he had helped many young boys and men to run away from the city. His wife gave me a black *chador*, and she taught me how to wear the veil in order to cover all my body and face so that no one would recognize me as an Armenian. Liana, like the other little children, only wore a small scarf on her head.

That night I stayed with Yeprem in the basement. We held each other very tightly. Liana, the innocent baby, was sleeping peacefully on the floor. I do not think that any adults slept that night. I realized how much I loved Yeprem. He was my only protection and security. What was going to happen next? Nobody knew. What was happening to all the other Armenians in the villages and cities, to our cousins and relatives? Yeprem told me that none of them wanted to leave the city. I was not crying aloud, but felt great sadness and fear of the unknown. I remembered the colorful snake killed recently in our house. I was telling myself that maybe that had been an omen. But I still was hopeful, as Dr. Eftekhar had told us that nothing would happen to us, since nobody knew about our presence in his house. Only he and his Armenian wife knew about this secret basement. Even his children did not know about it. He said the Turks would not stay long in the town and that they would leave soon.

I stayed the whole day with my husband in the basement. Now we were like the snake, living in a dark hole. We were not able to feel the warm sunshine and we were not able to see the beautiful scenery surrounding our city. But it was

temporary. We had each other and that was the most important thing. The wife of the doctor was very kind. She brought
us enough food and water for the whole day. When I learned
to manage my *chador* to cover my head without letting it slip
down, she told me that I should leave my husband and come
outside in order to breathe the fresh air, as my daughter
needed to be outside under the sun, to walk and run around.
I really did not want to leave Yeprem alone in the darkness.
But they insisted and said at least I should do it for Liana and
that I should not worry about Yeprem. I accepted and joined
the family. I was given the Muslim name of Fatimah. Liana
was called Leila. It was announced that we were their relatives who were visiting from a far.

Everyone was very kind to us. I learned how to pray like
a Muslim woman. Even Liana was imitating the women, and
whenever she found a piece of cloth, she covered herself and
pretended it was a *chador*. When everyone was sleeping, I
would hold Liana asleep in my arms. Yeprem would come
out to stretch his legs, smell the fresh air and visit his horse.
We would walk like new lovers under the dark sky, which was
lit with shining stars. We were not talking much. We were not
dreaming about the future as before. We were not even talking about Liana's future. Yeprem used to promise me that he
would give Liana the best education that existed anywhere in
this world. Now we were only discussing the present
moment that was given to us as a precious gift. Yeprem asked
me if I had heard any news from the household about the
destiny of the Armenians in the city. But I could not repeat
what I had heard from them. The news was horrible, and I
could not torture him with it. When our stay at Dr. Eftekhar's
house lengthened, his optimism started fading. One night he

gave me a small object twisted in a little piece of cotton. He told me to always keep it in my pocket. If something happened to him, or if I felt that Liana or I were in danger, I should give away all the jewelry and the gold that we had. But if that did not help, then I should take that object. He added that I should give the little piece to Liana and swallow the larger one myself. He said, "May God forgive us, I do not want you to be tortured and harmed by any one. I know our enemy, and I know all that they have done to our people in Turkey lately." He did not continue when he saw me crying. He held me in his arms and said, "Maybe God will have pity on us. I am so lucky to have married you. I will love you forever."

He would see his baby only at night. He would hug and kiss Liana in her deep sleep. We were afraid that Liana might say a word to the other women or children in the house and reveal our secret. I would see him only by the light created by the moon or a star. Every morning, before sunrise, I would return to my bed so nobody would learn our secret.

Little by little I learned of all the horrors happening to the Armenians of the town. They were saying the Turks had established their headquarters not very far from this house. The Persian government did not care what they were doing to the Armenians. As long as they did not bother their security, they were welcomed. The last king of the Qajar Dynasty was enjoying his life in the presence of an assortment of women and great luxury. He cared little for his fellow subjects, much less for the Armenians.

The Turks attacked all the Armenian houses. They separated the men from the women. Some of the local Muslim businessmen had taken the women to the *bazaar* so that the

Turks would not harm them. Although these brave people were trying to help them, in time the women were left in the open-air court of the *bazaar*, with almost no food or no hygienic facilities. There were many epidemics and the older women and children were dying fast. Some friendly Muslims either took all the young and beautiful girls into their homes, or the Turkish army abducted, raped, and killed them. The men, however, were immediately taken away. Most were taken to the mountains and killed, one by one, or en masse. Most of the time, when they found a man in a house, they first killed him in front of his family and then they took the women and the children away.

One afternoon, while sitting in a corner of the house and watching my innocent child take a nap, I was remembering our house and my family, worrying about their welfare. Dr. Eftekhar arrived in torment. He told his wives that the Turks finally had entered my husband's house. They had killed my father-in-law and taken my mother-in-law to the *bazaar* and had stolen all our valuables. Suddenly he realized that I was present in the room, but it was too late. I was crying without a sound. My *chador* was all wet, covering my face. He came to me and said, "Do not worry, I will protect you." I begged him not to say a word to my husband. What was the necessity for his learning the truth? The rest of the afternoon I cried and prayed that at least God would protect us.

I remembered that some weeks ago, Yeprem and his father had buried the most valuable objects from our house under the old tree, where the storks lived. But gold, jewelry and material possessions did not appeal to me. I wished that they had taken everything and left us alone. My poor in-laws, they were such nice people. And where were my mother, my sister, Kharse and her baby now? Were they also gathered in the *bazaar*? How were they living? I was no longer able to help them.

Every night Yeprem would ask me what the news was from outside. I would tell him little stories, but not the whole truth. I did not tell Yeprem anything about his parents. The only news I could give him was that I had learned that Andranik was alive. As they had promised us, he was marching with his army toward Khoy. While he was marching toward Khoy, he had learned Var village had been attacked by the Turkish army. So he decided to save them first. He still had time to arrive at Khoy to help us. But the battle took longer than expected, and when he triumphed in that village and started marching towards Khoy he learned it was too late to save Khoy. The Turkish army had already massacred the Armenians of the city. So he turned back to another mission and left behind all of us who had not run away and were waiting for his arrival, all alone and without protection, at the mercy of the Turks.

I wanted Yeprem to be hopeful and wait for Andranik. Maybe if he were hopeful, he could still find a way to save us. He only answered thoughtfully that it was taking too long, and I felt he had doubts about my statements.

Some days later, Dr. Eftekhar came home very upset. He told us that we should be very careful. The Turks had announced that if they found an Armenian man hiding with a Muslim family, they would kill the whole household, even the servants, and then they would destroy and burn their houses. Dr. Eftekhar was very upset. From that moment on, I felt that he and his wife changed in their attitude toward us. They no longer came with me to see Yeprem. They just gave me food to carry to him. Sometimes I would find them talking seriously. When I would approach, they would stop their conversations. When Yeprem asked me why they did not visit him anymore, I replied that they had gone away on a short trip.

One late morning when I was in my room, I heard loud cries and noises outside. I peeked behind the curtain and I could not believe what I was witnessing. A pregnant young woman with beautiful long dark hair was half-naked on the ground in the courtyard. She was crying and begging the soldiers who were surrounding her not to harm her baby. The soldiers were laughing and shouting. They were dancing around her. On each turn they were tearing a part of her dress. She was very advanced in her pregnancy. She was an Armenian woman who had probably just come out of hiding to ask Dr. Eftekhar to help her deliver the baby. But the soldiers had found her before she reached the house. Maybe I was there to witness all the horrors so that I could recall them today. Who knows how this world works? The soldiers were kicking her. One of them started jumping on her large stomach. I heard her last words-not to harm her baby. At this very moment another soldier took his large shiny sword and slit the pregnant woman's stomach from top to the bottom. She let a small cry and then she was silent. Many people were watching. But no one came to help. All were in shock. Blood surrounded and enveloped her in a red bed. At this moment another soldier put his hands into the open stomach, pulled a well-formed baby out and with his sword he cut the baby in two pieces and threw them at the face of the mother. The soldiers turned their backs and went to wash their hands in the little stream of water that was running at the curb of the

59

street, talking loudly together. They laughed and went away. I was sick. My body, my spirit, my whole being were frozen. I sat down. I was shaking. I was ashamed to be alive and to witness this. Was I going to have a similar fate? I was not afraid of the Angel of Death, I was afraid of the humans. At home nobody talked or ate all day, as if we were all respecting and mourning this unknown young woman.

One afternoon a few days later suddenly we heard a loud knock at the gate. There was much noise outside. I trembled and ran to Liana who was sleeping deeply. I took her in my arms and held her as close as I could to my heart. She woke up and looked at me with a smile and was reassured that I was near her. The servants opened the door. And suddenly I saw many Turkish soldiers so close for the first time. They looked human like us. There was not much difference between them and our men. How could they commit such horrors against our men, women and children? The man in the front had many medals hanging from his uniform, and it seemed that he was the commanding officer. He walked directly towards the secret basement and called Yeprem by his name. I was trembling, trying to hold back my tears because of Liana. He shouted that they had killed all the boys and men of the town. Yet here was hiding the most important figure of the city. I was hoping that Yeprem would escape through the back door. I was expecting a miracle, a cloud, and a hand that could hide him. But in a second Yeprem walked out proudly, holding his head high. For the first time since our exile from our house I saw his eyes and face clearly. It was not Yeprem anymore. He had deep wrinkles. His hair had turned gray in such a short time, and he looked thin and pale. He tried to look at Liana, his precious daughter, and he tried to smile at me. Suddenly, the commander and two other soldiers emptied their guns on Yeprem. He only cried loudly "**Ah**," and he died. The voice of Yeprem penetrated my entire being. His innocent red blood was flowing on the ground. I was shocked at this new scene of horror, holding my only gift left from Yeprem, my orphan daughter, Liana.

All the servants and the entire family were watching this atrocity in horror and shock. Dr. Eftekhar and his wives were standing at a distance. They looked less surprised than everyone else, but they also looked very sad. It did not take long for the soldiers to attach my dear husband by his legs to the tail of the horse that the commander was riding. He said this would teach all the habitants that they had finished their job in this city and that no one should leave any Armenian man alive. He turned his horse's head toward the gate and gave it a savage kick. When they were leaving, Yeprem's beautiful white horse arrived. He smelled the blood and ran towards the body. The soldiers left with loud cries of laughter and I watched them dragging my husband's precious body on the ground. His loyal horse was walking slowly behind them, in mourning.

I was just eighteen years old and Liana was only three. In less than an hour we had become a widow and an orphan at this very young age. I looked at Liana. She was calm, and with her innocent eyes she was looking at me. I held her with one arm and like a robot my other hand entered my deep pocket and grabbed the little rolled cloth that Yeprem had given me. I pulled it out while everyone was bringing water to clean up the blood and erase the human savagery. I sat with Liana at my side. I was sad, scared and in deep pain. I looked at this

61

angelic face, and I told myself that I could not give her the little piece of poison. Everyone loved her, and I was sure that Dr. Eftekhar and his wives would adopt her and raise her as their own. There was too much light and life in her eyes, I could not take this life away. Dr. Eftekhar already had all our gold and the jewelry in his possession. I thought that he would take good care of Liana. I looked inside the piece of fabric and saw two dark brown pieces, the size of my little finger. I kissed Liana goodbye and put the small piece of the brown object in my mouth and swallowed. While I was trying to swallow the second one, I suddenly felt a heavy weight on me. I do not remember what happened next. The sweet kiss of my daughter and a very bitter taste of the brown object were my only memories.

I do not know how many hours it took before I opened my eyes and found myself in a room surrounded by Dr. Eftekhar, his four wives and many other people. They held water in their hands. They thanked God loudly in Arabic that I had opened my eyes. They poured liquids into me, trying to revive me. Later, the doctor told me that he saw me putting something in my mouth and had guessed what it could have been. He had jumped on me in order to stop me from taking the second one. I had fallen down and become unconscious. He smelled the cloth and found out that I had taken opium. He had tried hard with his medical knowledge to save my life. I was crying and begging him to let me go. I told him my life without Yeprem had no meaning. When he was killed, I died, too. My soul also left my body with his when he cried his "Ah." But they did not believe me. They did not believe our souls left together. They wanted me to stay alive and take care of my daughter and be hopeful for the future. They did not know there was no future for me.

The Turks took all that I owned all that I loved so dearly. The Turks took my entire family from me. The last hope I had was Yeprem, and they took his life so savagely, too. They did not care I was standing there, or that his three-year-old baby was witnessing her father's assassination. They did not let him even say goodbye to us. They did not even let me have his dead body or a grave to cry on. The streets of the city became his grave. We learned later that his body had been dragged through all the streets of the city, that it had been destroyed little by little. Our horse had followed him until the end. When they found our horse several days later near our house, he was weak and tired. They tried to feed him but he refused. He died with his sad eyes looking at us. I lost the last possession Yeprem treasured so dearly.

Sometimes it seems nature and life is much stronger than the will to die. We always find a reason to survive. I thought if I stayed alive, I should not let Yeprem and all these atrocities be forgotten. When I finally got my health back, I was weak. They were taking good care of Liana and me. Liana was imitating the women by covering herself with *chador* and learning Persian words mixed with Turkish and Armenian.

Sometimes I would get upset as I was feeling that I was losing even my baby. What was the meaning of this life anymore? Why did we need to go through so many tragedies? Everyone we knew, our parents, our grandparents, all were honest and hardworking. We had helped everyone who needed us, and now we were in the hands of evil. Why?

Days passed. The streets were quiet. No one was making any noise. Even the soldiers were invisible. Early one afternoon when Liana was playing with earth and water, making mud pies; a soldier came in to ask for Dr. Eftekhar. They talked slowly and respectfully. Then the soldier went to the gate and waited there. Dr. Eftekhar came to me and said, "Do not be afraid. There is no danger for you or for your daughter. They know that since the death of your husband you are under my protection. They have promised not to harm you. The Chief of the Army is an old man, and he is a better person than the rest. He has to ask you some questions. Put on a *chador* and follow the soldier. He will bring you back home."

As I was leaving, one of his wives approached me. She took a handful of the mud that Liana had prepared and put some of it on my cheeks. She said that although he was a nice man, other young soldiers were around. I would better look dirty and ugly. She pulled my hair back and covered me with an old *chador*. I kissed Liana goodbye, as I was not sure if I would be back. I begged the doctor's wife to keep Liana as her own daughter. She kissed me and said, "Don't worry. You will be back."

I was praying they would not molest or rape me. If they wanted to kill me, I was ready to die.

We had a short walk as the Turkish Headquarters were near my house. I was following the soldier and looking around for the first time. The streets were empty. Some local people were uncomfortable with the presence of unwanted guests in their city. But the Turks were strong and the local authority was weak. When we entered the building, I saw an old man in the same army uniform worn by those who had killed my husband. I held my head down. The old man had a soft voice, and I was surprised that a human voice was coming from that uniform. The officer told me Dr. Eftekhar was his friend and he did not want to harm me. He added that he knew that my husband was very rich. He had heard he had a lot of gold. He just wanted to know where the gold and our wealth were hidden. I only replied, "*Boulmoura.*" [15] He said to think again and then answer. I replied that it was true that my husband was very rich. I knew he had many gold pieces. But, as you know, I said, I am his wife and I do not know anything about his wealth. The men do not talk about these things with their wives. I did not even know how I was going to take care of my baby. I was in such a miserable condition, and he looked at me with pity. I think my youth and my sad face had made him sympathetic. He said to go back to the house and stay there. He called a soldier who walked me back.

I was surprised at his kindness. How could a man of his character order all these brutalities? Did he know about the massacre or were the soldiers operating in chaos?

At home every one rushed towards me, and the doctor asked about my meeting. When I told him the commander had said he was his friend, he blushed and walked away. Since the death of my husband, they were avoiding facing me directly. Little by little, I understood the truth.

Nobody knew about the basement, they had told us. Neither their sons nor their most trusted servants knew of its existence. So how did the soldiers know where to go? I believe strongly that it was the doctor himself who had denounced us. I do not blame him. He had to protect his family. By giving away my husband, he had bought his family

---

15- "I don't know" in Turkish.

protection. Liana and I were included in the deal. That is why he was so sure they would not hurt me.

Dr. Eftekhar was very kind to us. He had been a good friend of Yeprem. My brother Nicola was the best friend of his sons. But our presence in his house was a constant reminder of treachery. I could see he was not comfortable having us around because I was sure he knew that I knew he was the one who denounced us.

After the assassination of Yeprem, we stayed for almost a year under the doctor's protection. One day he told me that he had received good news from my brother Nicola. He was back from Russia and settled in Tabriz. Nicola had sent a message that I was to be sent to Tabriz. This was one of the most important cities of Persia at the time, even more important than the capital. Tabriz, next door to Russia, was the main road to Europe. Nicola told me it would be better for me and for the future of Liana. Khoy was finished for the Armenians. But Tabriz could become a beginning, and maybe I could find the rest of my family if they were still alive. I was not used to making decisions. The first time I had spoken by myself was when I had answered the Chief of the Army. I asked the doctor to do what he thought was best for Liana.

He said he owned a peasant who was married and had many children. They lived in his village, and he had known this man since he was a child. All his family had been working for the doctor. He had complete confidence in him. In those days feudalism was the main agricultural system in Persia. A handful of rich people owned many villages. The mass of the peasant population was living under the power of the landlords. They worked hard even though they had almost no decent tools and the landlords were collecting all the profits. The landlords gave the peasants and their families little shacks to live in and barely enough food to survive. Wives and daughters would work in the landlord's house or they would weave Persian carpets without pay. Sometimes when they would see an extraordinary talent in a child, they would help him. The peasants' security and future depended entirely on the landlord, his kindness and generosity.

When Dr. Eftekhar said he had confidence in someone, it meant the person was really reliable. He said he was going to arrange a false marriage between the peasant and me. This way he would be able to accompany Liana and me to Tabriz with no problems. If we were stopped on the road, he would show the official papers that would prove I was a Muslim woman travelling with my husband and our child. He would find my brother and leave us with him. I would give our guide a piece of fabric to bring back so that the doctor would know that we were safe and in good hands.

I was listening, not saying a word. I could not even imagine what was expected of me. I was alive just to take care of my child, the only thing left from my husband and my past life. I asked him if we could go to our house to take dresses for Liana and me. He looked at me sadly. "Don't even think of returning to your house," he said. "Do not look back. Just look forward and start your new life."

By the next day, all was arranged. The peasant, Ali, was a middle-aged man. He did not even look at me. He promised the doctor he would take care of the baby and me. He said that we would be leaving the following day, early, before sunrise. The night before our departure the doctor called me to his room. He opened the bags that belonged to Yeprem and me. He pulled out all the jewelry and gold coins Yeprem had grabbed at the last minute. He said that he had spent a lot of money on us since we had been in his house and that he had to pay Ali and his family. He took much of the gold and jewelry. Handing the rest to me, he said I should hide it well. Attach it to my body under my garments, he suggested. Don't say a word about its existence to anyone, even after I was safe in Tabriz. This was the only security that remained for the future of my baby and me.

Early in the morning, I was ready to leave. I did not have baggage. Dr. Eftekhar's wives gave me two *chadors* and some dresses. They gave Ali food and water for the trip. The doctor paid him some money and told him, firmly, that he should do his best to protect us and return to Khoy as fast as he could.

I thanked them for their hospitality. We all cried as they followed us to the outside gate and watched us leave for our new destiny. No one threw water after us, as it is the custom to wish that the person who travels should return fast. Every one knew that this was a one way trip for Liana and me as there would be no return to this city anymore.

I did not even look at the city where I had been born and grown up. I had good and bad memories. I remembered when I used to tell my grandmother this was Paradise. She would always answer, "Hope that God will keep it always like this." Now I knew what she meant. This is the reason whenever they planned something for the future, they would always say, "If God wants." It is true. Who could tell us a year ago what was going to happen to us? Who could imagine that in a month I was going to lose everyone I loved my husband, my parents, in-laws, friends, and my house, all that I had? Now I was leaving alone with a three-year-old child, empty-handed, on the back of a horse with a stranger, into an unknown future.

Who could have imagined that I, the luckiest bride of the city, would leave this place as a widow, alone with an orphaned baby?

CHAPTER FIVE

Lessons of Nature

ॐ

We started our trip on horseback very early, before sunrise. I was riding the horse with Liana sleeping, attached to my back. I was feeling empty, as if my spirit had completely left my body. There were no thoughts in my head. No joy of life was present in my heart. There was nothing left for me to love or to look forward to. Liana was the only reminder of a lost life. It seemed that she had already forgotten her father's death. She was laughing, playing, eating and crying, like normal children of her age. I did not know when she would die like her sister and father. I was already dead. Just my empty body was functioning, my heart was beating, and my legs were able to move.

Overhead, the sky was clear. The sun was not fully up yet, but its light was already ending the darkness. I was not even looking back at the city. I kept my eyes almost shut. This was only the second time in a year I had come out of the house and the city. The only other time I went out of the doctor's house was when the Chief of the Turks asked to see me. For the first time, I was crossing the town. I cried quietly and said goodbye to the love of my life. I was crossing his tomb with every step of the horse. The Turks killed him, but they did not give us his body for burial. Now all the streets of Khoy had become his tombs, and my horse was crossing these sacred places. My tears were dropping down on the dusty road. Soon no one would ever remember that there were so many hard working Armenian families in this city that were destroyed by the Turks because of their politics or God knows for what reason. I was asking myself the famous question that has no answer: "Why? Why?"

Soon we left the limits of the city and started on a road through the mountains. The sun was rising, little by little. Its bright rays were penetrating the sky to banish the darkness. The sun's rays were penetrating even my closed eyes and were warming my cold body. When I opened my eyes for the first time, I saw the glory of the sunrise in mountains. It was amazing to see the red and orange colors of the sun and its reflection in the sky. Each moment the sun was rising, the light and the warmth were becoming stronger. The air was pure, and we were surrounded by silence. Sometimes I could hear the small song of a bird in the distance. I could see a little waterfall between the large stones where pure water was falling, making its way through the plants and stones. The music of the water was so relaxing. Liana was still sleeping calmly on my back. Ali was not talking or even looking at us. He only looked forward, opening the road for us to pass. It was as if he were not present at all.

I remembered my first trip with Yeprem. Unconsciously, I felt a little smile flitting over my somber face. But soon tears covered my eyes again. I was thankful Yeprem had taught me how to ride horses, even with closed eyes, as at this moment I was able to ride and protect his daughter and carry her out of the city. I was blocking my heart and mind from the past.

But the past was following me everywhere.

The mountains were standing so proudly, their heads touching the clouds. Nature was very rugged but beautiful. I did not know where I was going, but nothing could have been worse than what I had experienced lately. I thought that maybe I should be thankful that I was not raped or tortured and my daughter was not slashed into pieces like that other baby. I no longer asked about my mother, my mother-in-law, my sister, my grandparents, cousins or the rest of the family. All were counted amongst the dead.

Little by little, I could see little butterflies, lizards and even snakes on the road. Sometimes we could see a bird flying freely above us or we would hear birds singing all around us. Liana soon woke up. We found a little waterfall and a safe place to stop so the horses could rest, and that we could breakfast. Liana was calm and sweet. She was amazed and amused by her environment. This was the first time we were alone together. In the doctor's house, so many people were taking care of her that I was almost left alone and forgotten in my fears and sadness. Now she was alone with her mother. I had to become more awake in order to take care of her by myself. She ate her breakfast with a good appetite. Walking around, she talked to Ali and brought smiles to our faces. She reminded me of the sunrise that was breaking through the darkness minutes ago. She asked questions about where we were and where the rest of the people were that we used to have around her. When she went near the horses, she ran after a butterfly. She was amused to see a lizard. Suddenly I felt that by running after her and answering her questions, my blood, which was frozen in my veins, started flowing again in my body.

Here was an opportunity for a fresh life that was making everyone around her alive. Even the strange man smiled and told me she reminded him of his children. I was sorry to keep him away from his family. Politely, he said it was an honor to take us to a safe place. It would not take long to travel there. Then he could go back to his family. He was sorry for what had happened to us. After that, our relationship became more human. But we did not talk any more till the next break. We packed everything and started on the road again. I was telling myself that even the peasant had a house and a family that he would be enjoying in a week or two. But what did we have to look forward to? Where were we going to live? What were we going to do?

When Liana was sleeping, it was more comfortable for us. But when she was awake, it was difficult. She was sitting in front of me and I was holding her tight, answering her questions. She was speaking a mixture of Armenian and Turkish. When she was awake, we had to stop more often to rest. But when she was sleeping, we advanced faster.

In the evening we stopped at the entrance of a cave before sunset. Again the sky over the mountains became red, purple and dark blue. It was amazing to see the fight between the darkness and the light. I was standing in front of the cave, but amazed at the power of nature. Ali entered the cave to inspect it. He arranged a safe place for us to sleep. He assured me there was no danger. He had stayed in this same cave before. No thieves or dangerous animals were nearby. Sadly, he added that we had left the most dangerous animals back in the town. I took Liana's little hand in my hand and we walked in. The cave was still lighted with the sunset's reflection. As we were walking in, many birds, scared by our presence, flew out. Liana was happy to see all these birds and the calm and beauty present in the cave amazed me. Then I saw a big pool of pure cold water. Ali told me we could drink from it as it came from the heart of the mountains. I had heard in the fairy tales that there were youth and eternal life fountains in this world that people were looking for. This gave that same impression. I did not care to live long but we were thirsty, and we drank from the cold water. It was delicious and fresh, especially at that moment when we were tired and thirsty. Amazing stones and objects were in the cave.

After dinner, we spread our blankets to sleep. It was already completely dark. The little fire Ali had made was losing its power, and I could see the last fight that the little red light was trying to hold onto. Soon all was dark. Liana slept immediately. She was giving us no problems, as if she knew that we already had had a rough time and she should not add to it. I could hear little noises in the cave, probably the movement of insects or a bird. Who knows? Maybe there were other creatures present in this cave like the ones in the legends and tales. My eyes were getting tired, but I was afraid to sleep because every night my nightmares were coming back to me. My husband's assassination and the torture of the pregnant woman in the street were repeating in my dreams. I was amazed that I was not even excited about seeing Nicola soon. I was afraid to learn of more atrocities. I was ashamed I had not been able to protect our mother and sister, and I was ashamed to stay alive. But finally my eyes were shut. For the first time I slept peacefully, without the usual nightmare or the shouts in the middle of the night.

When I opened my eyes, I saw Ali was already up. He was

near the pool washing his face and hands, getting ready for his Morning Prayer. Muslims always must rinse their faces, arms and feet before the prayer. He opened his prayer cloth on the ground, facing Mecca. He put down the holy black stone with his hands in front of him and started praying.

Suddenly I felt a light in my heart accompanied by a sharp pain. I remembered God again. I felt my spirit was returning to my body. I had not really prayed after Yeprem's assassination. I had lost faith and hope toward everything, even God. How could God accept all these atrocities and injustices in the world? Why did God hear Abel's voice immediately and go to punish his brother? Was it because in those days only a few people lived on earth? Now were too many of us calling on him at the same time? When so many Armenians were dying in Persia and Turkey and so many soldiers, young and old, were being killed in Europe, how could God answer all these cries?

But this simple man, with his prayer, was awakening in me a lost presence.

Little by little, the purity of this man awakened my heart to goodness. Not all the human beings were savages. Not the entire world was dark. Still the light of God was shining on this world.

Hope traced its way through my heart and mind, and I started to appreciate nature more. I asked myself who was able to create a perfect world in such harmony and beauty. But then the second voice asked if the All Powerful could create these beauties, why could He not stop the cruelties and the injustices in this world.

Even right in front of my eyes Ali was the witness of another human injustice. He and his family were almost slaves. They were living at the mercy of their landlord. He and his family were working hard, and they were only getting enough pay to barely sustain their life. Their hard work was filling the pockets of their landlords with gold. His children were going to become peasants and servants of the capricious wives and children of the landlord. Why was God present in some places, absent in others? Was he promoting the evil men while leaving the good people alone without protection? It was difficult for me to understand all these problems. I was not able to reason why we were killed and destroyed as a nation. I was asking all these questions in my mind while watching the man praying, swaying, up and down. When Liana woke up, as soon as she saw the man praying, she took a piece of cloth and went close to him and started praying, imitating his movements. How could a three-year-old pray? She had learned from the women in the doctor's home. When she asked me why I did not join him in prayer, for the first time I heard myself saying, "Because we are Armenians and Christians. We do not pray like that." I made a cross on my face. I asked her to do so, and for the first time I repeated, "Our Father who are in Heaven." After the prayer I said, "Heaven is where your father has gone. One day we all will join him again." I could not continue talking. I felt my throat close up and there was no air to pronounce any words.

After our guide finished his prayer, we collected our little belongings, washed, ate breakfast and continued on the road. Liana was sitting in front and while I was holding her, we were conversing with each other for the first time. She noticed the birds and animals and plants, and she asked about them. I corrected her words in Armenian, and I tried to teach her new ones.

I was still sad and frightened, but I realized nature and life were more powerful than human sadness and tragedies. I started asking myself how many people and tragedies these mountains have witnessed. They had been standing there so many centuries. Did the stones remember the last words they had heard from a dying soldier? Did they remember the tears and the blood that fell on them?

Soon Liana fell asleep, and we attached her to my back. I was left alone. I had long days ahead of me in complete peace and silence. Now I was asking more questions. My sadness turned to anger. I forgot my miseries and I felt the anger about all the injustices in this world. I remembered the poor and sick people we used to visit with my mother-in-law. I was wondering what was going to happen to them now that we had left the city. The Armenians had been killed. But the Muslims, who would take care of them? I was angry because our horse had died; I was upset because the snake had died. I did not know where our storks were. Would they return next year to look for us, or would they not care who lived in the house. All these thoughts were tormenting me, but again a little bird's song or the touch of wind on my face would bring hope to my heart.

For three days we traveled in the mountains, far from people and villages. It was a kind of healing time for me. One day, suddenly, a thought penetrated my spirit. I told myself now that I am alive I am going to fight the best way I can. I am going to avenge the innocent blood shed in our city. I knew I would not enjoy life anymore, like a normal person, because of what I had seen. But I was not a normal person, either. At eighteen, no longer was I an ignorant woman. I had survived horrors, and I had a burden on my shoulders. The mountains and nature had taught me all these days. They had changed me into a new, stronger person. Arousiak, the lucky little bride, had died with her husband in the city. A new Arousiak had risen from her ashes. I started holding my head up proudly. I told myself I was going to help my daughter grow up so that one day I could tell the Turks, "You did not finish off all the Armenians. You tortured us, you raped us, you robbed us, and you killed us. But we kept our trust in God and in life, and here we are, witnesses of all your atrocities and ugliness. Are you going to be at least ashamed and regret your acts? Your words of sorrow and regret will be the only thing that I will expect from you in the future."

After crossing the mountains we stopped in the *carevansara* to sleep, and Ali brought us food and water. It took less than a week to go through all the mountains and villages, until we reached our final destination, the city of Tabriz, where I would be reunited with my sister, my brother Nicola and his family.

PART II

CHAPTER SIX

Re-Born From the Ashes

❧

Compared to Khoy, Tabriz was a big city. Streets were paved and there were well-kept houses, some very large, others quite small. They were made of brick and had gardens protected by high walls. People were walking in the streets or riding in carriages. Some men wore stylish suits, and some women were wearing *chador* or had only a scarf on their head. After awhile we came to a beautiful church. Ali took us to the gate and told me to enter and ask for the priest. I did not know how untidy I looked after so many days in the mountains. I entered the church and made the sign of the cross. Liana followed me and did the same. While I was approaching the altar, looking like a miserable Muslim woman with an old black *chador* covering my body, a young priest came out from behind the altar, looked at me and in a kind voice asked in Armenian, "How can I help you, my daughter?" Suddenly, I felt at home. After almost a year someone was addressing me in my own language. I told him my name and that we were looking for my brother Nicola. I told him where we came from, but I did not talk about the massacre. Looking at me kindly, he asked if I were the wife of Yeprem. When I answered positively, his voice broke. He said that they had heard about our sad fate and they were sorry for my daughter and me. He was sure that God would keep the spirit of Yeprem in peace. He had met Yeprem at meetings [16]. As if he were talking to himself, he said, "He was such a great man. It is a pity we lost such a rare human being. I hope God will give you and your daughter peace and joy in the future."

He placed his cross on Liana's head and he blessed her. I kissed the golden cross attached to a colorful scarf. Liana imitated me. As in all traditional Armenian churches, the smell of *khung* filled the atmosphere. We burn it in churches, in homes the night before festivities, and we pray and remember the souls of the departed in our families. For a second I saw my mother and my mother-in-law turning around the little dish that contained red charcoal with *khung* burning on it. They were spreading its smoke around and praying for the souls of the departed family members. Suddenly I realized that no one had prayed for the death of Yeprem and for the soul of all the other martyrs. I had not burned *khung* for my in-laws or my mother and for God knows how many members of our close family who had perished in the massacre. The voice of the young priest brought me back to reality. He told me he would show our guide how to take me to my brother's house. He said that he was aware of all the pain that we had gone through, but he added that God would help us find happiness again.

When we walked out, he showed Ali the way and thanked him for his hard work. After a short walk we arrived at a small

---

[16]- Mostly for perpetuating the Armenian language and religion for the Armenian students.

house. Within minutes the door opened and my brother Nicola came out. We could not believe our eyes. We hugged and cried. My younger sister ran to me. We hugged and kissed and cried. When I saw Nicola's wife, I was so happy to find her alive. We were hugging, kissing and crying at the same time. Liana was confused as she looked at these strangers. Nicola picked her up, kissed her and said, "I am your uncle." He said she resembled her father a lot. He was sure we must be tired. We did not dare ask questions of each other. I just said that I was sorry not to have protected our mother. He smiled sadly and said, " How could you help!" His wife immediately cut the conversation short. "Your mother died while I was trying to protect her," she said. I realized their child was missing. Nobody said a word about it, and I respected the silence.

My heart ached and tears dropped from my eyes. Poor mother. At her age she did not deserve to wander in the streets, hungry and cold, and die. After awhile we were quiet. Even the tears had dried. I still was wearing my *chador*, as usual. Nicola gently pulled it down from my head and said: " Arousiak, you are safe here. You do not need to be a Muslim woman anymore." Although Ali was not able to understand a word of Armenian, he also had tears in his eyes. Nicola thanked him. Kharse poured tea from the samovar. We were happy to finally drink hot tea from clean cups. They told us that there was a new public bath near their house. After resting, we could go there to wash ourselves. For the first time I was in a house that smelled like our old house. Kharse gave us some cake and filled our teacups again. Still nobody dared to ask any questions. We kept quiet and just looked at each other. Although we were all young, we all looked much older. The suffering had marked everyone's face. Nicola said Aghasi, our younger brother, would be back from Russia soon. Nicola paid our guide and said he could go to the public bath and stay in his house as long as he needed to rest the horses before returning to his village. When Ali gave him our marriage contract, Nicola tore it up in anger. I thanked him for his hard work and kindness, and I gave him the little cloth the doctor had given to me to return to him as proof of our safe arrival. The rest of the evening we stayed together not talking much just enjoying being together.

Liana and I went to the public bath. Since there was no hot water in homes in those days, everyone used the public bathhouses. Its steam and warm atmosphere made me relax after such a long trip. Liana was happy to play with the water. I bathed her, and while she was playing, I took off the three long pins from my hair, and gave myself a shampoo with a large bar of soap and hot water. It was so relaxing and comforting to have a clean body and clean hair. Liana was playing happily with water while I washed our dirty garments. Then I placed the clean, wet garments in a large towel and we rinsed ourselves for the last time with warm water. In the dressing room, I dressed Liana in her last clean dress while I put on my remaining dress. When I saw myself through the mist in the mirror for the first time in a year, I was surprised to see I still looked remarkably young and pretty considering my ordeal. My hair was long and fell freely to my shoulders. I remembered my engagement day and my wedding day. I heard all the women around me admiring my looks and my long hair. Tears filled my eyes but I controlled them immediately as I had decided not to cry anymore in the presence of others, especially Liana. When we returned home, my sister-in-law had spread a large comforter for Liana and me in one of the rooms with clean white sheets covering it. After dinner we all went to our sleeping beds. For the first time since our arduous trip ended, we could sleep in a clean and safe place. Ali stayed with us for two days, until the horses recuperated, and then he left us.

One evening when Nicola came home he found Liana covering her head with the cloth imitating the wearing of the *chador* and was praying like a Muslim. She had learned this from the women in Dr. Eftekhar's house. He got very upset. He pulled the cloth off her head and gave her a little tap. "Liana, you are Christian, and we do not pray like that," he said. "I do not want to see you with your *chador* anymore." Liana cried a little, but she never covered her head again.

I learned about the fate of our cousins and other relatives. We had lost practically everyone. But still we did not know the details. We were expecting our younger sister to talk. Then we would learn more because she had stayed in the bazaar with others. But she was not talking. Whatever news we had was coming from refugees that my brother and his wife had met. Some had gone through so much horror that they lost their minds and we were not sure what to believe. It was horrible to learn we would never see our mother, my in-laws, cousins, aunts, uncles, grandparents plus so many friends and neighbors.

My sister-in-law was holding up, but she had changed a lot. She was still a beautiful young woman but she had become more aggressive and hard. This was not the woman I had known. She finally told me one day that she was at home with my mother and sister and her daughter who was sick with a high fever. She did not know the reason, as she was afraid that my sister would be infected. So she sent my sister to our cousin's house. For some days nobody came after them, as they knew that her husband and brother-in-law were out of the country. She started crying. She was trying to cool down the temperature of her daughter but nothing was helping. The poor child did not even have the strength to talk or to move. Kharse said all the time she was remembering my daughter Lousik and she knew deep in her heart that she could not save her daughter. She continued in tears and said, " I was not even able to call a doctor. With all the money that we had, I was not able to do anything for her. Our child died within two days, so fast that I could not get help.

"I buried my little child with tears in our garden under the old mulberry tree that you liked so much." She cried harder. Nicola had tears in his blue eyes but he was not saying a word. His eyes were looking far away. I hugged Kharse and said, "I know your pain. I am aware of your broken heart." Suddenly I saw our two little children with angelic smiles looking at us from above. Kharse said that, as it was getting dangerous to stay in the house; one of the neighbors came and took her and my mother to the bazaar. They said it was the safest place for the Armenian women. "The bazaar was filled with the women, children, mostly girls, and little boys dressed up as girls. There was no comfort and food for all these women and children. It was getting cold at night. We were all sleeping close to each other on the cold ground to keep ourselves warm. Before we left the house, I had taken blankets, and I was hiding my jewelry and gold under my large skirt. I gave coins to the merchants to bring food that I would share with others. When they saw that I could pay them, they started charging more and more for a smaller portion of food. Then your mother became ill. She started with a high fever. Many refugees got typhoid fever and other diseases. It is amazing; I do not know how I did not catch any of those infections. The living conditions and the hygiene were so bad that they were life-threatening. The women, young and old, with the little children were dying every day. Sometimes their dead bodies were piled in a corner. The smell, the dust and the whole situation was miserable. It was not helping the sick women and children to heal.

My mother-in-law's condition turned from bad to worse. Upon our arrival, when I saw that living in the bazaar was so uncomfortable, I told my mother-in-law we would not stay long. I would take her to one of Nicola's friends' house so that she would have some comfort in her old age. After the death of our child she was weaker, more in tears and heartbroken. She was trying to hide her sadness from me. When she became infected and started to run a high fever, there was no way anyone would accept her in that condition in their home. I was carrying her on my back, moving her from one place to a better place, looking for sunshine and heat. But running away from the *bazaar* was very difficult. So I decided to stay until she got well. Her condition did not improve. Her fever kept rising. Delirious, she was begging me not to abandon her. Delirious with the high fever she was repeating that if I left her alone, the dogs would eat her. I reassured her that I had always loved her like my own mother, I would never abandon her. After days of burning with fever and suffering she died in that horrible place. I did not want to leave her body in that cold and dirty *bazaar*, so I gave some gold to a young merchant and asked him to prepare a proper burial for my mother-in-law. He promised he would arrange it that same evening. I asked him to bring me a *chador* so I could be present during the burial. I promised to pay him more when he accomplished all this. That evening he told me that he had arranged the burial. We left the *bazaar* in the dark and buried her in a farmland, far from any homes. He accompanied me back to the *bazaar*. As soon as he left, I decided not to enter into that hell anymore. Death was present everywhere. I was not afraid of it so I decided to challenge my destiny.

I decided to go back to our house and see if I could hide or die in my own home. At least I had my child's body there. I had abandoned her in that cold earth all alone. If I had seen your sister, Zarouhi, in the *bazaar*, I would have stayed with her. But I never found her in that chaos. I ran away with the *chador* covering my body. Sometimes I had to tighten it around my waist so I could jump over the walls and the roofs of the houses, like a cat, jumping from one place to the other. Finally I arrived home. Our house looked the same as before. No one had entered yet. It was cold, dark and silent. There was no child calling "mother," and no members of our family were walking around taking care of each other. It was sad. I burned a little candle and went to the grave of our child. I hugged the humid earth. I kissed it and cried.

I do not know if I passed out or slept on her grave till the sunlight woke me up. For a moment, I was not sure where I was. I vaguely remembered the events of the past days. I was not even sure if they were dreams or reality. Gradually I realized the truth and tears covered my face. When I returned to the house, I heard soldiers' voices. They were breaking down the gate. I ran to the basement, entered the dark oven and closed the lid. I do not know how long I stayed in there.

The Survivor

Then I heard noises in the basement. The soldiers were eating the bread that was piled up near the oven. It seemed that they were searching in the dark. Then I heard someone approaching the oven. A soldier opened the cover. I was squeezing myself against the wall of the oven. He stuck his hand in the oven and moved it around. I felt his hand touching my hair. I saw my death approaching. But after a moment, he closed the lid, and he told another soldier in Turkish that the house was empty. Then they left the basement. I do not know how long I stayed there, as if frozen, in the oven. When I came out, it was dark and quiet. I was tired and hungry, so tired that I slept or maybe fell unconscious on the floor again. When I opened my eyes this time, I saw the Khan. He was trying to help me wake up. I was confused and stood up immediately.

We all knew the Khan. He was a very rich landlord in Khoy. He owned numerous villages. Peasants and their family members had worked for Khan's family for centuries. He was also a friend of Nicola. He had seen the gate half-open, therefore he had entered to see if the women were alive or needed help. When he learned all that had happened from Kharse, he invited her to his large house. Kharse said they were kind to her but all the images and horrors followed her regardless. I told her that I could understand her as I had seen and heard about a lot of atrocities while I was in Dr. Eftekhar's house. Who would have predicted all these tragedies a year ago when we were all drinking tea under the large tree and talking and laughing with each other? We were crying and were trying to comfort each other, saying that at least it was over and we did have each other.

When Nicola came back from Russia and learned that his

wife was alive, he had asked the Khan to send his wife to Tabriz.

My poor sister-in-law. She had lost her daughter, her mother-in-law, and all her belongings in just a few days. Although the Khan was rich, he had taken most of my sister-in-law's jewelry and gold upon her arrival in his house, pretending that she was too young and people might steal them from her. He promised that later he would return her property, but he never kept his promise. From Kharse's entire family, only a sister and a brother who were in Russia at the time of the massacre were left. Later she learned from her younger sister that the Turks had killed their father, two brothers and her brother-in-law in front of her sister with an axe because they had said that it was a pity to waste their bullets on Armenians. They had been married only a short time.

I soon realized that Kharse had changed a lot. Who would not after all that she had gone through? She was bitter and ruthless, with no pity for herself or anybody else. This was not the woman that I had known.

I knew that we were a burden on Nicola and his wife, but I did not know what to do. One night, we began talking about Khoy again. Suddenly Kharse said, "You never told us what happened to all your jewelry and gold. Don't tell me that you were not able to bring anything out with you." Nicola felt uncomfortable. He said it was too early to ask, but she did not give up. I told them exactly what had happened. My sister-in-law asked me to show them what I had kept. I could not refuse her. After all she was my older brother's wife and he was like a father to me. He was all I had. Nicola was quiet. I did not think that he approved of her behavior, but he did not dare to contradict his wife. She had become bossier and colder.

The pain had weakened my brother. He was feeling guilty for having left the city and was thinking he could have helped everyone more. I went back to my room and closed the door behind me. I remembered Dr. Eftekhar's words; he had said that I should not show my remaining wealth to anyone, even my brother or sister. I pulled out some gold coins and jewelry. I put them in a handkerchief and hid them in the corner of my blanket. Then I opened my secret pocket that was attached to my waist and put it on the table. Kharse pulled the bag toward her and emptied it on the table. All the gold coins and the jewelry covered the table. For the first time I looked at them and was amazed to see the Russian Tsar Nicolas's head on the coins. They were large pieces. She told me, "Bravo that you could carry these heavy pieces all this time." Her eyes were gleaming in a greedy way, and she immediately started grabbing the coins and arranging them in little piles.

It was almost a month since we had moved in with my brother and his wife. One day I asked Nicola if he could help me find a room to rent and if there was a possibility of me finding a job. He started to say that it was too soon to discuss it, but his wife cut his words short and said, " I know a place not far from here. The Armenian Relief has opened a small office in order to help the refugees. They are looking for a woman to work with them. I will take you there tomorrow."

I was surprised at her reaction. In the Middle East, we are famous for our hospitality. We used to have guests in our house for months and even years. I had been in their house for only a month, and she was trying to get rid of us. I thought, well the war had not only destroyed lives and killed people, but it had transformed people and their behavior. I told her I would go the next morning, hoping for a chance to find a job. I noticed that her eyes were fixed on one of my necklaces. I gave it to her and said, "You have done so much for me and Liana. I would like you to have this."

Nicola opened his mouth to say that I needed it for the future of my daughter but the necklace was already around her neck. I was neither sad nor surprised. I had seen so much of this wealth and I had seen the end of my life. The gold and jewelry did not interest me. Unexpectedly, Kharse brought out a small box and arranged most of the gold inside it "You are too young to keep this with you," she said. "It is dangerous to carry it, even under your garments in the secret pocket. People will cheat you and steal from you. I will keep it safe for you. When you need something, just ask me and I will give it to you."

I was not able to protest. Who could deny her older brother's wife something in those days? I looked at Liana sleeping peacefully in the other room and felt pity for the poor orphaned girl. Nicola looked pale and ashamed of his wife's behavior, but did not say a word.

ٿ

CHAPTER SEVEN

A Working Woman

ॐ

The next morning after my encounter with Kharse, I woke up early, made breakfast for everyone and was ready for the job interview. My sister-in-law took me to the refugee headquarters in a modest building. All the people there were the survivors of different villages. We all resembled each other, poor, weak and without anything or anyone. Everyone had lost family members, houses and belongings. Everyone used to be someone in his own village. Now we were equal, all refugees. The Relief Center was organized with the direct help from Americans. They were the ones who were donating their time and money to help the refugees and the orphans from all over the neighboring cities and villages.

They hired me with a very small salary. Liana was allowed to stay with me most of the time. She was a joy to the people around her who had lost their family members and their own children. I rented a room in a nearby building, close to my brother's house and to my work. Although it was unfurnished, I felt that it was better for everyone that we lived apart from Nicola. My sister-in-law was also happy to see us settled. I asked her if we could have some of my gold pieces to buy the necessary furnishings for our room. She said that was not necessary, she would give us some drapes, linens, blankets and china to start with. I thanked my brother and his wife for their hospitality and moved to our new room. It was a small, sad place. But seeing all these miserable people I was forgetting my own problems and trying to help them with theirs. At least I was young; I had my daughter and some money. There were many people less fortunate than I. Some were old and had lost everyone. Others were tortured by Turks and were not able to forget. We knew the soldiers had raped some young girls but they were not talking about it at all. A few of these girls were carrying the unwanted child that would remind them of the horrors for a lifetime; these pregnant young girls were half-dead and quiet. Our job was to help everyone and find them food, a roof and jobs.

My sister visited us often. I could not believe that such a young girl had changed so much and looked so much older.

One day finally she started crying and telling us all the horrors she had gone through. She was playing with our cousins in their garden when the Turk soldiers attacked their house. The boys ran to their mother and she went hiding behind a large tree. As she was a tiny girl, none of the soldiers had paid attention to her. She was crying louder and louder as she told her memories. We cried with her. She stayed behind the tree so long that she slept there all night. Early the next morning when she woke up, she saw the door to her home was open. When she called and heard no answer, she entered and saw our three cousins, boys between eight and twelve years old, with their feet hanging from the ceiling. They looked horrible. Their pink faces had turned blue, and the smell was unbearable. In the next room she found our cousin dead on the floor; her blood had dried on the carpet.

Motionless and speechless, she stood there. Why had these people done this to our dear cousins?

My sister continued, "I did not see their parents. Suddenly I felt a strong hand grabbing me. After that I was not afraid or surprised of anything or anybody. Nothing mattered any more as I had already met the Angel of Death."

She said that the local Muslim population had thought that the *bazaar* would be the safest place for Armenian women. They had closed both ends of the entrance of the *bazaar* to the Turks, and they were protecting the women. The neighbor took her to the *bazaar* and told her that she should stay with the others. She would be safe there. She saw some little boys dressed as girls. This was how the mothers were protecting them from danger. But then she had seen women and children dying from hunger, disease and cold.

My little sister was only twelve and-a-half years old. She had seen so many horrors. At her age, I was getting married and being treated nicely. My poor sister. She had been hungry, dirty and cold and suffered so much during the war. I pulled her toward me and hugged her tightly. I felt pity for her. At her age she was an orphan and had nothing. She had all these awful memories to live with. I was happy that at least she was able to tell us the horrors that she had kept for such a long time. I told her that if she wanted, she could come and live with Liana and me. I told her that all would be better in the future. Our parents were watching us and would help us. In tears she asked: "If they were going to be with us, why did they leave us?" I had no answer. Nicola said that his house was more comfortable and it was better for her to stay with them. I was surprised that Kharse also insisted that she stay with them.

A *working woman*

With the smallest noise my sister would jump and ask who was coming now. Later she came to visit me and we used to go visit her. I had a lot of pain seeing my little sister. She had no freedom. She was almost like a maid in her brother's house. She worked hard, scrubbed and did the laundry. I understood why my sister-in-law insisted that she stay there.

A year passed and we heard more horror stories. But time was healing us as usual. Everyone was getting used to this new life. As hard as it was, we were alive.

છ

CHAPTER EIGHT

A New Sad Chapter

❧

I was still working at the Armenian Relief Center. With the little money that I was earning I had decorated my small room. Liana was growing up among all the different people who had come from neighboring villages and cities. She was talking to all of them. Her language skills were amazing, especially for her age. She had learned poems and songs in different languages. When I was too busy, others would take care of her and I was reassured that she was in good hands.

Sometimes important meetings were held in the Center. Most of the Armenian dignitaries came to these meetings. One day they were expecting two very famous *Fedaiis* for a meeting. The atmosphere in the Center was like the old times in our house when Yeprem had his secret meetings. But now, nothing was secret. I was working in the office when two men entered. Both of them greeted me and said that they were grateful for my hospitality. I was confused. They said that they had been in our house for meetings many times and they had seen me from a distance. They knew that my mother-in-law and I prepared all the food and meeting rooms for them, but they had never been able to thank us. They told me how sad they were at the loss of Yeprem and all

96

that had happened to our city and to our family. But they wanted me to know that Yerprem's acts had helped many families. I should tell my daughter that Keri and Karo told me that her father was a hero who died for his people. It was an honor to see these two famous Armenian soldiers. I was happy to know that my husband had had an impact on peoples' lives, although his wife and daughter had lost him.

One day I saw two tiny girls, a boy and a woman entering the Center. My heart stopped. I was happy to see my old friend Nasik, her sister, her younger brother and her mother, Banafsheh. We hugged, kissed and cried for awhile. But it was great to see that they were alive. Later Nazik told me that the Turks had entered their house, each of them hiding in a different corner. They had found her two brothers who were about eight and ten years old. They had pulled them out and told them that they should follow them. She said that her older brother had fallen down. The soldiers ordered him to stand but he never did. Later they found out that he had died from fear.

The soldiers had taken the younger brother with them. Her mother was crying and did not know what to do. The next morning her mother asked their Muslim neighbors to help her bury her older son, and she asked friends to find her younger son. He was too young to be taken away. After three days a woman called them and said that her husband who was a shepherd had found her son naked in the mountains. Banafsheh and the girls with some other women had gone to the mountains where they found the naked boy sitting on a stone. Banafsheh covered him with a shawl and they brought him back home. The boy did not talk for days. Later he had said that while the soldiers were taking him along with some other boys in the streets, he had overheard them saying that they should kill them but another soldier had said that they were just kids and not to harm them. While they were arguing, he and another boy had decided to run away as nobody was able to see clearly in the dark. So they ran toward the mountains. But he did not remember what happened next until the shepherd found him. Banafsheh said that he should not torment himself. Their Muslim friends had helped them and recently they were able to leave Khoy.

Nasik was a reminder of my good times. As always, she was sweet and calm. It was a pleasure to meet her again and enjoy her love and respect.

Liana had a friend who lived with her mother across the yard. The two children usually played together in the yard for hours. Either her mother or I would watch them. One day I told my neighbor that I had to be absent for an hour if she would watch the children. We never locked our rooms with keys as the neighbors watched each other. No one, had any valuable objects in their houses, we were all refugees. Living in a small room with few belongings. When I returned that afternoon Liana was still playing in the yard with her friend. As soon as I entered in our room I realized that some one had gone over my belongings. My blue handkerchief was on the floor. The only valuable object that I had with me was a wallet of Yeprem. He had bought it in Armavil while he was studying there. He always carried it with himself. I had saved some money in it. It was a valuable object for me, it did not have any market value and the money was not much either. I always kept the wallet in a clean handkerchief, its presence meant a lot to me. I immediately understood that the wallet was missing. The only one who could take it was Liana, her friend or her mother. I was very upset, I ran out and asked Liana if either she or her friend has gone to the room. She told me that they had been playing outside all the time she had not seen any of the neighbors. She had once seen her friend's mother entering our building. I had tears in my eyes. I never cried or cared about all we had lost but this wallet was different. I went directly to my neighbor and asked her to return my wallet. I told her that she could keep the money but only return the wallet. She started screaming and told me that she had never entered our room in my absence. Suddenly she tore her blouse and pulled out her naked breasts. She rubbed them against the stone stairs that we were standing and said, " I have fed my child with these breasts, I ask God to punish the real thief and take away the child of the person who has stolen your wallet." The children were watching amazed. I trembled with fear and I felt a chill in my body. I had never scene such a seen. I asked her in tears to leave the children alone and cover up. I walked to my room sadly with tears and with fear. One week after this incident her beautiful daughter died from a sudden illness. A week after the burial, she moved out of the building and we never saw her again. Liana and I were very sad. We never forgot this event.

One day Khoukas, Yeprem's youngest cousin, entered the office. I was surprised to see him because we thought he had been killed. He was the only male who had survived from Yeprem's entire large family. At the time of the massacre he was fourteen years old. He told me his sisters and his mother were also in Tabriz and they would love to see me. Later we went to visit them. We hugged each other and cried. Khoukas told me that one afternoon his father came home very sad and told everyone to get ready to leave. He and his father dug a hole on the ground. They put a large wooden box inside and filled it with all their valuables. They covered it with earth and put bricks on top. Later that evening they walked out slowly, following the wall so no one would see them. After some time they arrived at a Muslim friend's house, owned by his father's best friend. They were guided to a large room where there were already six other families present. The women stayed in that room. But the men had to climb a ladder so they could hide under the roof. After some days the soldiers came, pulled the men out and took them away. The Turks killed his father. But his mother, her two sisters and the rest of the women were taken to the *bazaar*. Before the Turks arrived at the house, Khoukas was the only male hiding in the basement of the house and no one had found him. After four days, when he walked out to find food, the friend of his father was happy to see him. He asked him to hurry into his house so nobody would see him. After a week, the soldiers came back and asked for him.

The Muslims circumcise the males immediately after their birth, but Armenians do not. This was a big difference between Armenian and Muslim men. But Khoukas was born circumcised. The Muslim friends of his father knew about this. They used to tease his father and say that Khoukas was born a Muslim and he belonged to them. So the Muslim friend had told the soldiers that they had converted Khoukas and even had him circumcised. The soldiers asked to see proof. Khoukas said shyly that he was very embarrassed, but they urged him to show proof. Finally he pulled down his pants and when the soldiers saw the proof, they even kissed him and left the house. He stayed with them till the departure of the Turks from Khoy. Later he found his mother and sisters who had suffered while staying in the *bazaar*, and they moved to Tabriz. They had lost all their wealth, but at least they were alive and united.

Most of the refugees would get together. Some would repeat the horrors and their losses and some would listen and look far away, as if they were lost in the past. These were the ones who were alive physically but were living-dead. We would get together to cry. Then one day everyone realized that regardless of all the tragedy, life continues. We stopped talking about our past. Everyone tried to find a job and start a new life.

ﻉﻼ

CHAPTER NINE

A New Marriage

❧

One day Kharse invited us to her house. She told me to wear my nicest dress as she had some important guests. That night only one man had been invited. He was nice looking, and I immediately understood their intent. I was angry and thought, "How could they?" I did not speak to anyone at the table and after dinner I went to the kitchen to help my sister who was working so hard in the house. She told me she had overheard our brother and his wife planning my wedding with the man who was named Avak. That night I was very upset at my brother and his wife. Because of my anger and sadness, I did not sleep. How could they forget and try to replace Yeprem? He had been so good to everyone. My heart belonged only to him. I did not have an empty place for anyone else. I had gained a little independence and self-confidence, and I was managing my life very well. At night Nicola and his wife came to visit me. They told me that Avak was madly in love with me. He had asked for my hand from my brother. Nicola added that Avak had been in love with me in the past. Before I married Yeprem he had asked for my hand. But as Nicola had to choose between him and Yeprem, he refused Avak.

A New Marriage

Now there was a different situation. I should remember I was a widow with a child and not many men would like to take on such a responsibility. They said Avak was a decent man with a good job. How long was I going to work and live in such a small room? Liana needed a father. He would become a good father to her. So my brother had given Avak his permission to marry me. I started crying. Although Tabriz was a modern city and there were girls' schools and women were more active, women still respected an older brother. His words were final. We were not able to refuse him. I cried. I said that I could not marry anyone but Yeprem, he was the only man in my life. Kharse told me with a sad smile that nobody asked me to forget him, but that I should start a better life for my daughter. Later, as days went on, I would love him, too. The main argument was that I could not stay a widow all my life.

They arranged my wedding with a man whom I did not know or want. It was a very small ceremony in the same church that I had seen the first day of my arrival in Tabriz. Controlling my tears, I asked Yeprem in my heart to pardon me. I told him that he was my only husband and only love.

We had a little dinner in my brother's house with some members of both families. It did not seem like a party or wedding for me. It was a sad evening. But as my mother had said, I was the family's honor and I had to play my role. After dinner they kept Liana who was half-asleep in their house and told us that we needed a free day for ourselves. Liana cried and I went to her bedside to comfort her. Soon she closed her eyes and slept like an angel.

Avak had prepared a nice little house for us, and he had moved all my belongings to our new house. Nicola had given him some of my gold as a dowry so that he could use it for my daughter. As soon as we arrived home and he closed the door he rushed to me like a hungry vulture and said, "For years I have watched and desired you. Finally you are mine." He smelled of alcohol; his face had changed and he looked ugly. He pushed me into our bedroom and tore off my simple wedding dress and with no respect or love, his hands went all over me and he consumed me like a savage. Then he turned his back to me and soon I heard his snoring. I cried quietly all night; I was not able to compare this savage man to my real husband. What had my brother done to me? How was I going to accept this behavior every night? How could I live with such a man when I held Yeprem always in my heart? I felt guilty and ashamed, disrespectful towards myself. I asked thousands of questions and finally I reassured myself that probably, as it was his wedding night, he was drunk and had overreacted. Tomorrow would be another day and probably he would become a better person. I was so tired physically and mentally that I fell asleep. I was not asleep for a long time when I felt his weight again on my fragile body. I was not raised to refuse. I had to obey my husband.

After breakfast he looked very satisfied and happy, like a conqueror. His attitude hurt me a lot. When he left home I was released. I knew at least that I had some hours for myself alone. I cried and felt miserable. Avak was a nice person in the presence of other people and a rude brute when he was alone with me. In the afternoon Kharse and my sister came to visit me. They brought Liana with them, as she was impatient to see me. When they saw my condition they asked me what had happened, but I could not describe it. My sister cried with me without knowing what had happened, but

Kharse told me that I should be patient and all would go well in the future.

Some weeks later my brother, Aghasi, returned from Russia. He was working with Nicola and was still single. At least his presence was a comfort to my sister.

My life continued sadly. I was living with a stranger under the same roof. I could never call him a husband or a friend. The gap between us was getting larger and larger. I never asked him what he did with all the gold that my brother gave him. I was doing all the work by myself, but he never had a kind word or a compliment for me or for the delicious food that I was preparing. I was only praying to God that I would not have a child by him.

One day when my sister came to visit me, she looked sad and I asked her the reason. She said she was crying for our parents, and she was not able to forget our mother's last days. She asked me why we all did not die with her. She said we were still suffering so much and that she was not able to see any hope for a better future. I comforted her and gave her one of my hidden jewelry pieces; a nice carved gold necklace that looked like fine woven lace. It made her happy but it brought me new problems. When Avak and Kharse saw it, they asked me where it came from. I told them that I had kept a souvenir of my past for my daughter Liana. But, since my sister was an orphan and had nothing left for her, I gave it to Zarouhi instead. Both asked me what else I had hidden from them. The conversation ended there. But after that day Avak searched everywhere. One day, I realized he had found my last pieces of gold and jewelry that had been left for me and my daughter from Yeprem. He took all the gold and jewelry without even asking me.

The Survivor

One day Kharse told us that she had decided to travel back to Khoy. As Nicola had many influential Muslim friends, she would see if she could recover some of our belongings. She said she would see if she could sell our houses and bring some money back for all of us. She asked me to sign the necessary papers. I could write my name, and I was proud to add it at the bottom of the papers. Travel conditions were much better, and this time she found the trip comfortable. Nicola also had gone back to Russia on business.

When Kharse returned from Khoy, she told us that our house had stayed intact. Dr. Eftekhar had protected it for us. But nobody offered the real value for the houses, as they thought that we would never return to Khoy. So she sold them at very low prices and brought some money with her. I asked her if she was able to dig under the large tree and find the objects Yeprem and his father had hidden. She said she had seen nothing. But months later I recognized the Yeprem's colorful hat. He always said that his great grandmother had sewn all the colorful work on the hat with very fine needles and that it was a very valuable item. Kharse never gave me any money. When I asked, she told me that she would keep the money. Seeing my situation with Avak, she would give it to Nicola to add to his capital, so that later we would all have more money.

One afternoon I heard someone calling me. I opened the door and saw Nazan. I was surprised because we had not heard from her since the killings. We hugged each other; I invited her in and prepared tea. She was the wife of one of Yeprem's cousins, a nice woman. Before the Turkish attack on our city, she had three daughters, between the ages of one and four. I did not dare ask questions that I knew would touch upon another sad chapter in our lives. But while she was drinking her tea, she started telling me her story. She said that when she had heard the cries of her neighbors, she had taken her daughters and gone to the basement where she covered herself and the children with old rags. Her husband had gone to Russia for business. Since the roads were closed because of the war, he was not able to return. Later she had heard that he had become ill and died near the border. She and the girls stayed in the basement for days. But it was hard to control the children since there was no food. She had never cried but had decided to survive regardless.

One day she saw that the face and body of one daughter was covered with red spots, and she was burning with fever. Even when she gave her all the medical aid she could, the child did not stop crying. Again she heard the voices of the soldiers around the house and since her child was noisy, she put her in the pool [17]. Thinking that her fever would stop in cold water, she put her hand over the mouth of the child in order to stop the loud crying. When she felt the soldiers had left the neighborhood, she took her hand off her child's mouth and pulled her out of the pool. Only then did she find that her daughter was dead. She buried her in the yard. That night her husband's Muslim friend, Masht Agha, had come to check on them. When he saw her alone with the little girls, he offered to take them to his house. At any moment another soldier could break into the house.

She said that he had a large house, several wives and many children. They gave her and the children a room. After

---

[17]. In Persia, most houses had a small pool in the yard. The Muslims had to immerse any food or object in the water three times before its use, in order to make them *hallal* and clean.

falling asleep, she was awakened by the presence of Masht Agha in her bed. When she tried to resist him, he said, "If you make a noise, tomorrow morning you and your daughters will be thrown in the street." She had to protect her daughters. She had no choice. The wives of Masht Agha were very jealous and mistreated her. They forced her and her children to pray with them three times every day. She learned their melodies, and she would sing with them by using Armenian curses instead of their words. She said they had to stay in that house for one and a-half years, until she was able to contact the Armenian rescue group and ask for their help.

While listening, I was amazed at how she had changed. How could she retell the story so indifferently? Was the savagery a contaminating disease? Had we caught a virus from the Turks? Were these men and women like this before the massacre or did the massacre change them? I remembered her as a nice person but now I saw a stranger in front of me. Then I remembered the Chief of the Turks that I had met. He seemed to be a good person. What the soldiers did, was it human nature or was it from orders coming from higher up?

I did not believe that the Chief had ordered the two soldiers to slash the pregnant women in the street. I did not believe he ordered them to attach Yeprem to the tail of a horse and drag him through the streets. These events were the result of the savage desires of human beings.

In my heart, I felt distant from Nazan. In the past, I had respected her. She had always been invited to our house for special occasions. I was happy to see her, but deep inside I was shocked. She asked me how my life was but I did not say much. I had learned not to complain. God had given me a destiny and I was trying to adjust to my situation. I asked

Nazan to stay for dinner. She accepted and said she should have brought her daughters so that they could play with Liana. When Avak came home while I was preparing the table, they started conversing. After dinner while I put Liana to bed, I left them alone. When I returned, I saw that she was sitting very close to him. As usual, he was half drunk and did not know what he was doing. Later she asked him to accompany her to her house, which was not far from our house. While I washed the dishes, I thought again of Nazan and all the people that I had met in Tabriz. I was amazed at their transformation. Avak came home later than he should have. I thought that he had met a friend or stopped at a liquor store for a drink. Tabriz was situated in the northwest of Persia. The weather was very cold in winter. This was an excuse for men to get together in a liquor store that served drinks, mostly vodka, with little appetizers. This was a favorite place for Avak.

From then on Nazan came more often to our house, mostly when Avak was present. Sometimes she would bring her daughters and say that they cried and asked for Liana. And sometimes she would come by herself. Little by little, I felt that something was happening between her and Avak. I was not jealous, as I was not in love with him. But I was raised with a respect for purity of the family. What they were doing was adultery, which was prohibited by the Ten Commandments and by our religion. Again I kept my silence. At least I was left alone and in peace most of the time in my bed. They became more involved, carrying on even in my own home.

One morning when Nazan came to our house she told me, "You work so hard all the time, today I will prepare the coffee for you." As she insisted, I let her do it and I played with the children. After an hour, I started feeling a strong pain. I was not able to move. At that moment Nicola, who was back from Russia just that morning came to visit me with his wife. Seeing me in such pain, he offered to take me to the doctor. But Nazan said it would pass, as I had been very healthy that morning.

They stayed, and as my situation was getting worse. Finally they took me to Doctor Lam, an American doctor who was practicing in Tabriz. As soon as he examined me he said to Nicola that apparently I had been poisoned and that they should transfer me to the American hospital next to his office. I was hospitalized for two days; they placed tubes in my stomach and washed it out several times. I was so weak and the doctor told us if we had not gone to the hospital in time I would have died. They tried to find the cause of the poisoning. But it was not apparent and I was not suspicious.

When we returned home, I found out that Nazan had stayed in our house in my absence, pretending she was there to take care of Liana. Once at home I felt that I was not able to trust this woman anymore. She pretended to be so affectionate and kind to me. Kharse said that as soon as they returned home, she would send Zarouhi to come and stay with me and take care of Liana. But Nazan immediately proposed that she stay and watch over Liana and me.

Avak was worried about me, and he was trying to be kind. I felt that Nazan had become irritated that night. Liana was already sleeping and I had closed my eyes. When they saw me asleep, they left our bedroom. Later I heard Nazan and Avak talking and arguing in the next room. I slowly walked out of my bed and put my ear against the door to hear what their argument was about. From the little keyhole I saw her filling a large glass of alcohol for Avak. In a low voice she said, "You keep quiet, even if you do not agree, you have to accept it. The only way left for us is to eliminate Arousiak; she is an obstacle for us. This morning I gave her a small portion, but I do not know why her brother came. If not, we would be free by now. Liana would be no problem, either." The man was drinking, and his silence was his approval. I trembled, not for my life, but for Liana's. I had not saved her from the Turks in order to offer her to a cruel-hearted Armenian.

In the morning, when I felt a little better, I dressed and told them that I had to go to church to pray. They had a mocking smile on their faces. I took Liana and went directly to the church where we had made our union. I asked permission to see Serpazan Hayr Melick Tangian who had known Yeprem and our family. He was the most important figure of the Armenian Church in the entire state of Azerbaijan. He was the same person who had sent the telegram to Yeprem in Armenia. I was not sure that he would receive me, but I had been forced to aim that high in order to save my child. He received us graciously, and his holy face gave me comfort. He asked me kindly what the occasion of our visit was. I was surprised to hear my own voice. "I am here as the wife of Yeprem, asking you to annul my marriage with Avak or I will disappear with my daughter into the mountains," I said. His face became somber and he asked me to tell him everything. I cried as I talked. Liana pulled at my skirt and she also started crying. He told me to return to my brother's house and he would take care of the problem. At the end of the conversation he told me that he had a picture of Yeprem when they had gathered for an important educational meeting. But I never asked him to show us the picture. This time I returned to Nicola's house completely empty-handed. They received us kindly. Later Nicola was called to the church with Avak and the divorce papers were arranged and signed. He was supposed to pay me back all my fortune that he had taken. Kharse had the official papers in her possession but I never received anything back from him and I never saw him again. I never mentioned his name and our union to anyone. But this time I promised myself that I would never marry again and will stay the widow of Yeprem, as long as I live.

The affair between Nazan and Avak did not last any longer, as my presence in the house had been their protection. Without my presence the community would learn the truth and would badmouth Nazan. Soon after Avak left for Russia. We never saw or heard from him again.

ॐ

CHAPT ER TEN

Alive, but Dead Forever

❧

Soon I looked for a job again. I was lucky as I heard that the American Doctor Lam was looking for an employee. When I presented myself, he remembered me and I was given a position helping his wife with their children and, when needed, with his patients. I helped his wife very little with the cooking and housework. I was mostly busy taking care of the children. It was perfect for me because they had offered to let me live in their comfortable house with Liana. As I did not have any belongings, they gave me all we needed. They were kind people. I was hoping that Liana would pick up some English words. I learned a lot from the doctor by from being present in his office with his patients. I was reminded of my mother-in-law who had healed people. One day when I told him about my past experiences with natural medicine, he became interested and asked me many questions.

A year passed; everyone's life was getting better. Liana started school, and I had to rent a room for her from Kharse who now had a bigger house and was renting rooms to people. Doctor Lam's house was too far from the school. My sister moved in with me as the three children of Kharse had grown and were going to school, too. Liana walked to school with them. While she was at school my sister worked in a garment factory on a sewing machine. In the evenings when the children would return from school, Kharse and Zarouhi were present to meet and feed them. They would do their homework, play and sleep. I came home only on weekends, as I had to stay twenty-four hours with the Lam family. In return I was able to pay our rent, buy food and new garments for Liana, and pay the school tuition. Many times I would be also useful to Kharse and help them by doing the very large laundry and cooking. I was not worried about Liana as she had her aunts and cousins to stay and play with. Zarouhi had worked very hard for Kharse; she had taken care of all the children and had received no salary. Now she could make some money for herself for the first time.

One day while Kharse was visiting us; Liana came to me crying. She said that you have told us not to work on Sundays and in the Adventist school she was attending, they were closed on Saturdays and had school on Sundays. "It is okay if I go to school on Sundays," she said. "But they forced us to sew on Sundays. When I refused to do that the teacher got upset."

Kharse told her not to cry. She said, "Nicola has received an important contract. If he succeeds, I will pay your tuition and you will be transferred to the American school." Three days later she came back to our house and told Liana happily that Nicola had succeeded in his deal. As promised, she could now go to the American school. Liana was very happy.

Later the young priest whom I had met in church, Ter Karapet, a handsome and bright person, asked me to marry him. In the Armenian Church priests can marry; only the ones who decide to reach the higher position of *Serpazan* are not permitted to marry. I refused him politely, saying I would never marry again. I closed myself to all the pleasures of this life. I belonged only to Yeprem. This time nobody forced me to marry; my brother was feeling guilty about what had happened to me.

Soon my dreams came true. Liana started reading and writing in Armenian, Persian and English. As I had decided with Yeprem, she was attending the best existing school for girls. She was a bright girl, and I was hoping that one day she would become a nurse. I was fascinated with the doctor, how capably he treated his patients. He always said that I was becoming a nurse myself. I would tell Liana all about my work and dreams on Friday, the only holiday that we had during the weekend. I would tell her about an Armenian midwife who had studied in Russia and helped women have babies. But for a girl in Tabriz, becoming a doctor was unrealistic. At nights in my spare time I would make lace to sew on Liana's dresses because I did not want anyone to call her a poor orphan.

As Liana was growing up, she asked me about her father. I told her he went to war and was imprisoned in enemy hands and that one day he would come back to us. I never talked about my past to anyone, and I had asked my family not to remind me of the past. They all respected my wish, as everyone wanted to forget the past in order to move onto the future. I only told Liana that her grandmother was a very generous person and that she resembled her. I was not able to help her with her homework. I hoped she would study hard. I told her that she should be the best in her class.

Years passed, Doctor Lam and his family finished their

mission in Persia and left for Italy. We were all sad at their departure. We had become like a family. They asked me to move with them to Italy. But I refused. How could I leave my sister and brothers. They were all I had. He introduced me to the American Hospital, and I worked there for many years. I moved back to our house and lived with Liana and my sister. My life continued between my work and my home. By now, my entire being was dead. I was only alive to take care of Liana. I never looked at a man and I never dreamed of another life. I was hoping that once Liana grew independent, Yeprem would come to take me home.

Sometimes we were invited to a friend's house, for happy and sad occasions. When there was a bigger party the only time that I could not control my tears was when someone would sing the famous Armenian song *Kroung*. This song talks of the migrant bird and says, "*Kroung*, you who are coming back from your trip, I am thirsty for your voice, give me the news of my country..." I would see my own storks in front of my eyes. Our large tree and everyone happy talking under its shadow. Then the image would fade and I would find myself alone, a widow in a large city among people who pretend they are living and enjoying life.

My brother, Aghasi, finally found a nice much younger girl and married her; later they had four children.

Years later, my sister met a veteran Armenian soldier who was proud to tell everyone that he had fought under Dro and had been wounded in the war. He would show us his trigger-finger proudly, the place that the bullet had gone through his hand. He had been married once but his wife died years ago and he had no children. He was much older than my sister was but he asked her to marry him. My brother agreed and they got married. I do not know if at the beginning she was in love with him but they made a nice couple. And later they had three children. My sister was such a calm and obedient girl, that she would accept any fate without complaint. I believe that we two sisters had learned to live without complaining about the life that was given to us. Maybe this is how our mother had taught us.

One-day Nasik invited us to his brother's wedding. It was a simple wedding. They had asked permission of the church, as the bride was only thirteen years old. The laws had changed by then. The bride was Nazan. I knew her from a distance. Since she had been back from Khoy she had lived with Banafsheh for a year. Banfsheh said that she could not keep two young people under the same roof and watch them; it was better for Nazan to marry her son. Then I learned her story. She was at home in Khoy with her father and the two brothers. The Turks came and took her father. They killed him in the nearby mountains where they had a large hole ready for many Armenian men who were shot there and thrown in. Her mother tried to escape with her sons, but they were found and killed. Years before her father had rescued a young Muslim boy who was an orphan and kept him with his other children at home. They had protected him under their roof and had treated him like their own son. Actually this was the person who had informed the Turks of the hiding place of the entire family. They never understood how that boy could be so deceitful after all they had done for him.

Before Nazan's mother ran away with her sons she asked her neighbor, a nice woman, to take care of her daughter, Nazan, who was six years old. The neighbor was a Muslim woman, married for a long time, but with no children of her own. Her mother knew that they would take good care of her daughter. She lived with them seven years after the massacre. They took care of her but also used her as a maid.

One day Nazan heard that they were planning to marry her to a Muslim man. At that time Banafsheh had returned to Khoy in search of family members. She knew that many girls were hidden in Muslim friends' houses. Persian Muslims protected most of the women who survived. Some of them left immediately after the Turkish soldiers' departure, these were the ones who were respected and protected by real Muslim friends. Some had lost their freedom and were not able to leave the people who had protected them for different reasons. Some Muslims believed if they converted a Christian to Islam they would directly go to Heaven. Others were molesting young girls. The girls were ashamed and did not know how to face their community.

Banafsheh was a distant relative of Nazan's parents. Although Nazan was only six at the time of the massacre, she had always remembered her parents and the ugly memories of the past and had never forgotten her identity. She visited Banafsheh in secret and asked her for help. Banafsheh knew everyone because she had baked bread for many families for years. She gave some money to a truck driver and told Nazan to be at the station very early in the morning. Nazan stayed awake all night so she would not miss the truck. She ran away from the house and went to Tabriz. The people who took care of her were not happy. They went to court in Tabriz and accused Banafsheh of stealing Nazan from them.

Later they summoned Nazan and Banafsheh to a hearing in court. They placed her alone in a large room where there were some military officers, a judge and a priest. One officer opened his jacket and showed her his bullet belt. "If you lie, I will shoot you with all these bullets," he said. "But if you tell the truth, you will go free." They asked her if Banafsheh had stolen her from her adopted family. She said, suddenly she heard a loud voice coming out of her body replying with a big "no." She added that "I am an Armenian and I want to stay Armenian. The adopted family wanted to marry me to a Muslim man and to convert me to Islam. That is why I had asked Banafsheh for help." They told her she was free to go.

Liana was growing up to be a beautiful young girl, and she had many friends. Times had changed; girls and boys were dating secretly. They were going to parties and dancing. Many boys were attracted to Liana. She danced the tradition-al Armenian dances beautifully and also all the modern dances that the boys and girls now danced. I was telling her all the time that she should only think of studying, but she was able to both study and enjoy life. Sometimes she complained that when she came home a little late Kharse put a lock on her door. She told her she was being punished because she should have come home immediately after school. My sister also told me that she would be inside the room and Liana was locked outside. Both would sit near the door and cry. But she never dared to open the door or say a word to Kharse. Liana complained to me for other reasons. I knew she was right, but I had no choice. I would say that she should respect her aunt, as she was older.

When Liana was sixteen, she met a young man at my sis-ter's birthday party. His name was Bacrate, a handsome boy. He had just graduated from the best Armenian high school in Tabriz. The level of education in that school was equal to that of any college. He was teaching at a school in a nearby village. A sensitive person, he also was a poet. They fell in love, and it became a nightmare for me. I wanted her to finish school and then marry, but she wanted to marry the man of her dreams. We talked and argued for months, but nothing could be done. They married when she was sixteen and he was twenty-six. I cried instead of being joyful.

I now realize I made a major mistake. I worked so hard to pay all the bills and buy whatever Liana needed. But she had been looking for a solid and secure shoulder to lean against as she had always felt like an orphan. She always was a lonely girl. She had a house that I had given her, but instead of a loving and present mother there were aunts and uncles who were taking care of her. But they could never replace a mother. Her aunt had been there to punish her when she was late. Kharse never did that to her own daughter and sons because she said she was responsible for Liana. If something would happen to her, she had to answer to me. I did not blame her. On the contrary I have always been thankful that she was there.

I realized again that we were all paying the consequences of the war. If Yeprem were alive I would have been with Liana at all times and she probably would not have looked for a man to marry at such a young age.

A year after they married, she bore a daughter and they called her Seda. I became a grandmother at the age of thirty-three. From that day everyone called me "Metza" meaning grandmother in Armenian. I always wore black or dark brown clothing and I pulled my long hair into a knot. A year later, she was pregnant again; this time she had a son and they called him Hrayr. One day while Liana was feeding her child she showed us a newspaper and read it aloud. "You see some soldiers have been found," she said. "They are looking for their families and are free to go home. I hope, soon we will read that Yeprem is free from prison and is looking for his family. Soon my father may come back home, too."

Kharse was also present. She asked me what Liana meant. Liana told her innocently that when soldiers are freed from prison, they look for their families. Since her father was captured during the war, she was hopeful that one of these days he would return home. Kharse got very angry with me and said, "Were you crazy to keep your daughter in the dark for all these years? How could you do this to her? Give her the peace that she needs." Then she told the girl the whole story. For the first time Liana cried over the death of her father.

ﻉﻝ

CHAPTER ELEVEN

Second World War

❧

Liana was having a hard life. I was living alone and still working at the hospital. This way I was able to survive and help my daughter economically. The political situation had changed in Persia. Now it was called Iran. The new dynasty was called *Pahlavi*. Reza Shah was the King of Iran. He wanted to modernize the country. He tried to abolish the *chadors* and give women their rights. If a woman had a scarf on her head the police would take it off her head and would tear it. He was trying hard to modernize Iran. But outside the country, it was also the beginning of the Second World War. After seven years, Liana gave birth to another daughter and they called her RoseMary. When RoseMary was six months old the Russians attacked Tabriz, and we all left the city. Later we all moved to Teheran, the capital of Iran.

I lived with my younger brother and his wife as they told me that it was not good to live with a son-in-law. But later I understood that as my brother and his wife had small children, they needed help, so I was the best option for them. I moved with all my belongings to their house. I worked all day helping his wife clean, cook and take care of three children. I was not paid a salary, which was normal. I was a sister eating at their table and living under their roof. But in reality, I was being used as a maid.

Iran did not enter the war, but was touched by its consequences. Soldiers were stationed in Iran. We could feel the war and live with it from a distance. I was reliving in my mind the dark periods of the Armenian massacres. I felt and saw all the horrors every night in front of my eyes and heard the "Ah" in my ears. Now instead of Armenians, they were killing the Jews everywhere. People would joke in the lines for food and would say, "The soap that we are buying is made from Jewish fat in Germany." Some would look horrified and some would laugh. I knew exactly what was going on. Someone would wear my necklace and the friend would say, " Well this is *Hallal* as it comes from a non-Muslim. Enjoy it."

I could hear the Jewish children crying for their mothers and fathers, but no one wanted to accept that such things were happening. I could see women being separated from their husbands, fathers and brothers and I would say, "Well I know what you are going through. If you remain alive you will become another Arousiak. Everyone would take advantage of you, telling you that they are doing you a favor, because you lost your status and your loved ones and because you were hurt. You will never forget what you have seen. Your peace will come only when the Angel of Death visits you one day."

In Europe people were suffering because of the war. In Iran we were suffering because of its effects on the economy. Food was scarce. We had to stand in line in order to buy bread, sugar, almost anything. Many people were unemployed. Life was hard on everyone. Some merchants would accept credit and sell bread or other food to the customers.

They would say, "You will pay us when you have money." They trusted the customers. In most cases, they did not even have a book to register debts in. This kind of solidarity and friendship that exists in the Middle East is common, especially among the people who believe in God. The most famous teaching, which is still practiced in Iran, says, "You do good deeds and throw them in the Dagleh [18], God will help you while you are in the desert."

Bacrate was working for a British company in their food warehouse, as controller and accountant, far from the capital. Everyone was taking advantage of the chaos after the war. The soldiers from all over were stationed in Iran: Indians, British and Americans. The company supplied all the food and goods, which were being shipped to different allied military bases. Bacrate was telling us that many employees were profiting from the situation and were stealing from the warehouse. He was disturbed. Bacrate was an honest person, and he stayed that way all his life. One day when Liana was visiting her husband, his friends and co-workers came to her. Complaining, they asked her to influence her husband to let them take advantage of the situation. They told her that when they shipped sugar bags to different locations, if they shipped forty-eight kilos instead of fifty kilos, no one would realize the difference. But two kilos from each bag would bring a lot of money in the black market. They could all share it with him. He did not need to do anything, just write that there were fifty kilos of sugar in the bag. They said that Americans and British governments were so rich that they would not care even if they lost a kilo, here and there. They

---

18. Tigris River.

reassured Liana that if Bacrate cooperated with them, they would take care of the rest and then Liana would have more money to take care of her children and could live comfortably. It was so tempting for Liana since she was not very rich. But when she brought the subject to her husband's attention, Bacrate asked her sadly, how she could even dare to repeat what they had said. Bacrate never would work dishonestly, although there was no one present to check on him but his conscience. His co-workers found other ways to cheat and steal from the warehouse. After the soldiers left Iran, his colleagues started spending their stolen money. They became rich and bought many large houses but it never impressed Bacrate. They had even told him many times that he could have had all that and even more if he had listened to them. Bacrate always said that it was true that if he had stolen two kilos no one would have known it, but he could never face himself in his life if he had joined them in their actions.

Much later when there was a strong earthquake in Iran, where the earth had opened up a large triangle and swallowed villages around Teheran; we all felt the powerful jolt in the city. For days, the people were practically living outside in streets. There were many fatalities and destruction. Some months later I bought kilos of rice in the store. When I was cleaning it, I found a small paper inside the rice. It was nicely printed in a foreign language. I gave it to RoseMary to read for us. It said, "From the American government, to the Iranian victims of the earthquake."

Later when I looked at the large, beautiful houses, I asked myself which one of them had been bought with the stolen rice money!

When the soldiers left the country, Bacrate lost his job

and was unemployed for some time. After they spent all their savings, Liana began knitting pretty sweaters. I do not even know how she learned to knit so well. She had many customers, but like Persian rug weavers, she was working hard all day and was knitting day and night. But the buyer was paying only for the wool and a small amount for her hard work. It was the law of the country, all the less fortunate population was working hard and a handful of people were living in luxury with their families, enjoying life. At least when we were rich we cared for the people who worked for us. But now everyone was thinking only of himself.

Liana was proud and did not complain. Maybe she was feeling guilty at not finishing her school. I was also angry with both of them. Why did they not wait until she finished her education before marrying? Three children with little money was a difficult situation. Sometimes we would pass by the houses of Bacrate's old colleagues and Liana would ask me, "Who is right and who is wrong?"

When the war ended, things started changing. We could see the results of malnutrition on our children. Seda was sweet and quite a young beautiful girl. She was a good student in her class and she had grown quite tall in a year. But she was thin and pale. Soon she became ill and was not able to go to school. Liana tried hard to help her daughter. She took her to all the doctors that she could afford. Medication was expensive and she had to wait in lines for hours to buy a simple pill. She was taking care of Seda and her family in the mornings and knitting late at night. She had to borrow more money for the cost of medication and later for the hospital expenses. But Seda's condition was not improving.

I decided to move in with Liana and her family. I was still

a strong woman. Everyone had taken advantage of me and they had taken all my belongings from me. The only thing left for me was my energy and love for my family. I felt guilty that I had been too young to protect my daughter and all that belonged to her. Now to make up for the past, I decided to give myself completely to my daughter. I had always thought of my sister and brothers. Nicola had done so much for us that I always felt guilty and I always tried to pay back and do the same for my other siblings. I felt pity for my younger sister and brother that they did not have their mother and father, we had always helped each other like an extended large family. But now I had woken up and realized that by doing so I had abandoned my own daughter. I felt guilty that I had not been able to see clearly. I decided to dedicate the rest of my life to my daughter. I left all our differences and egos aside. If she had married too soon or had not continued her studies, that was history. I had to help her from now on. I cooked and cleaned and helped my daughter as much as I could. I told stories to my grandchildren, made little toys out of cloth, taught them our traditions but never told them about the war or the past.

Seda was not getting better. I cooked the most nourishing foods I knew. I used all the healing that I had learned. In order to give her strength. I made chocolates out of butter, eggs, sugar and cocoa. Everyone loved and ate them, but Seda would just put a small piece on her lips. She was not even able to swallow for a long time. I powdered the shells of eggs and gave them to her in her milk. I beat egg yolks with sugar until it turned white. After adding hot milk and cocoa, I begged her to drink. But Seda was getting weaker and weaker. My heart was aching. But I had to keep a happy face for the rest of the family. She remained calm and quiet. When all the girls her age dreamed of boys and their future Seda asked a friend to bring her the homework so that she would not fall behind in her class. We were counting her days and she was waiting for the end patiently, without complaining. I took care of Hrayr and RoseMary while Liana took Seda to doctors and hospitals. Finally the doctors said that she had tuberculosis. It was better for everyone that Seda should stay in the hospital where we visited her every day. Antibiotics were rare in the country. But they were giving her the necessary medications, and she looked a little better after she was admitted in the hospital. One afternoon when I went to visit her, I found her bed empty. The nurse came to me and said that the night before Seda had received her dinner and had eaten with a good appetite. But when she returned the tray to her, she thanked her, as always, with a smile and closed her eyes. She never opened them again. She was only sixteen.

On the day of her funeral, I looked at Seda's peaceful face. I saw Lousik in her arms. Our hearts broke again. This time it was too hard to see my daughter suffering from the depth of her being. I knew her pain, and I knew that she would carry this wound as long as she lived. I tried to comfort her. But I was heartbroken myself. At nights I cried for my lost dear ones. I stayed with my daughter; we cried, talked and we cared for each other. Then we learned not to cry together in order not to hurt each other more.

Life continued. For me the only time I felt free of the all burdens was on Good Friday, the night of observing the crucifixion of Jesus. They would decorate the church in black; a wooden coffin would be placed in the middle of the altar. All

night the priest would pray and talk about Jesus and his sufferings. I would go to church and stay awake all night. I
would cry for my past, my present and my lost life. I would
ask God all my questions. Somehow, knowing that Mary and
even God's son suffered would give me strength to go on
with my own life another year.

I focused my love on Hrayr and RoseMary, because I knew
they were the only hope left for all of us.

Bacrate started to teach again and this was what he loved
to do the most. He would bring all the notebooks home and
would correct every word with his red pencil. Looking at his
nice handwriting, I would think that his students were lucky
to have such a great teacher. He would write poems and he
was the editor of a children's magazine. But his salary was
always pitiful, like all teachers. He was heartbroken from
Seda's death. He published a poem in the newspaper that
everyone cried over and talked about for months. The title
was "Sweet Sixteen".

Years later, he was chosen as the principal of an Armenian
school in Ahvaz, in Southwest Iran, Liana decided to stay in
Teheran. Hrayr and RoseMary were studying in good schools.
She did not want to disturb them. No one would stay in
Ahvaz in the summer anyway. The weather would get hot and
humid and there was no air-conditioning. Traveling back and
forth was not easy. So they decided that Bacrate would travel
and live alone during the school year in Ahvaz. As soon as
school was over, he would return home.

During his absence we would communicate only by letters. Sometimes friends would come to bring us little gifts
and good news about his successful work. He added classes
every year, offering excellent schooling. When he arrived

home, Hrayr and RoseMary would jump all over their father, kissing him and opening the gifts he brought home. He always brought chewing gum, candies and cookies. It was a pleasure to see the children happy with their father.

At night when the children went to bed, I stayed with Liana to talk, cry and share her pain. I knew that the loss of their daughter had made a deep bond between the two of us. We were working and living, but we were lost in our pain. Bacrate was working a lot and every one was praising the great job that he was doing at school. During summer vacations, students and teachers would come to our house to visit. The teachers and students loved and praised him. By this time Liana was working with a French dressmaker and was sewing beautiful dresses for Queen Soraya and the wealthy society women. She had to replace the absence of her husband at home with her children but my presence and my help also comforted her. At least her mother could be with her at all times. She had missed her mother and father while she was growing up, but now at least she was able to feel close to her mother.

For Liana and I there were only two choices left: either become bitter and get angry with everyone and remember our loss and cry for it, or look forward to life, forgive everyone and smile. We chose the second option. Liana never became bitter with her past. She carved Seda's image in her heart and put a large smile on her face. People would come to Liana and say that they envied her happiness. She helped and loved everyone. She forgave all the family members who had taken her possessions or had mistreated her. Every one called her the mayor of the family and of our neighborhood. Anyone in the family who had a medical problem or faced childbirth would first come to our house and Liana would go with them to the doctor or to the hospital. She would stay during the entire labor, if it took an hour or days. When my sister Zarouhi underwent surgery for her gallbladder, she stayed with her at the hospital day and night for an entire week to watch over her I.V. and other needs. All the children in our family were born in her presence, with her encouraging the mother and holding her hands. The doctors were happy to have her around. If someone would get in a fight with his wife, husband or friend they would come for advice and comfort to our house. She never asked about the wealth that her father had left. I always told her that I made mistakes and people took advantage of my widowhood, but at least she had me. Money and gold were not all there was to life.

I also forgave Nazan. There were so few of us left from an entire large city; that bitterness had no place in our hearts. At least she was a reminder of our glorious time and of Khoy. Soon after her affair with Avak, Nazan, like all the remaining survivors, worked hard all her life to help her daughters grow up and receive an education. I always felt that her actions were due to what she had faced in Khoy. Some reacted and behaved the same way as their oppressors. They became hard and evil. Others never changed. They stayed good regardless. But at the end, everyone went back to their original molds from which they were made. They became the persons they were before the massacre. What Nazan did to me, her past actions and choices were her problem, not mine. I never told her or anyone else about her relations with Avak and my poisoning. We visited each other, ate and talked with our daughters and their children. Our children and grandchildren continued their friendship.

131

The Survivor

When RoseMary became older and learned about the past, she would sometimes say, "Grandma, how can you forgive and love all these people who have harmed you?" I would answer that the past belongs to the past. The people did not mean what they did. The events had turned them into what they became. Now they have changed. Besides, you cannot cut off all your relatives. They are your blood. It is good to keep your relationship with all of them. Just forgive and accept them as they are.

Nasik married, had a daughter and lived not far from us. Her husband died very young. She lived with her daughter until the end of her life. We visited each other once in awhile; she always respected me and treated me as before. She was the only person who could help me regain the happy moods of the past. I loved her because she was a good person. She remained good, regardless of her hard life.

Years passed and my grandchildren grew up. I encouraged them to study and do their best. I did not have money or gold to give them, but I had my hands with which I could prepare the most delicious foods that I could, to love and hug them as much as I could. I realized that I had not given all this to Liana, because I had become a mother and a widow at too young an age. I was just working hard to sustain life and pay the bills, and probably I was working even harder to stay busy all the time, so that my mind could not travel to the past. I was upset because my daughter had not studied and had married so young. In reality I started realizing that I had remained in deep mourning all these years. I had stayed calm and strong, avoiding any talk about the past. I thought that if I do not talk about the horrors, and if I ignore my sorrow, the memories would fade eventually. I was mistaken.

Now I understood that I had accumulated so much pain in my silence. I had stored them deep in my heart. Although the dust of time had covered them completely, but then the smallest event would uncover this deep wound which was still very fresh. Finally, I accepted that I would never be a complete normal person as much as I live. I was like a bird, which did not have wings to fly or legs to jump with. I missed Yeprem very much. I knew that if the Turks had not killed him, the kind of life we would have lived. We were given a chance to live in this world this one time, and what a turn our lives had taken because of crazed politicians. How many lives were destroyed and for what reason!

We all missed a great future because of a meaningless massacre. If their goal was to finish off the Armenians, well, they did not achieve that, as there are more Armenians now than in our time. They created chaos and every one became evil in this chaos. Even friends and family members took advantage of the situation. After the massacre most of the widows and orphans were looking for protection and help, they went towards their family members who were more fortunate. Instead of protecting them, they took advantage of their needy relatives. They built their future by using the remaining money and the physical strength of the refugees. It was too late to return to the past and change the events. I had been so oppressed by my family members, our traditions, and our society that I could no longer start a new life again. Instead of blaming and hating the Turks that caused us all our miseries, I was blaming myself, I was blaming my innocent daughter and I was blaming my destiny. What had I done to be blamed? How could I forget all the horrors that I had seen? How could I forget Yeprem's *voice*? How could I forget the pregnant woman? For the first time, I felt pity for myself instead of being strong or searching excuses. Now years had passed.

Finally I tried to overcome my past grief. A ray of light started penetrating my spirit, it was the light of hope that my two grandchildren were shining on me. I started seeing some of my dreams and hopes accomplished through their actions. I found unconditional love, deep in my being. I was filled with love that I shared with my daughter, her children and with everyone regardless of whether they were kind or unkind to me. Now I owned nothing, I had no possessions; I only had love and respect to share with everyone.

Sometimes our relatives would ask me to cook a complicated meal. They would all say that my hands were different from theirs. They would say that whatever I cooked was delicious and theirs was not. Some meals we would eat together with all the extended family, meals like *khash*, *harrisa*, and the soup of the sacrifices. When someone would get sick or survive an accident, the family would sacrifice a lamb or sheep. The butcher would come to the house and give the name of the person who had healed or had escaped a dangerous situation. We would say a prayer and he would slaughter the poor animal. The skin belonged to the butcher while the rest of the animal was divided, placed in plates and offered to the neighbors, relatives, and friends and to the poor families in the neighborhood. The children would take the plates to other families. This was a way to teach them to share. A part of the meat would stay with the family. It was cooked in water with a little salt and pepper. At the end we would add freshly chopped parsley before serving. This was consumed as a spiritual meal, simple, but it had a very distinctive taste. All these foods were served at noon. In Iran we always ate one big meal at lunch. For dinner everyone would eat yogurt or fruits with bread. Dinners were only served for weddings and parties. *Khash* was the most complicated food to make. It needed a lot of preparation. I would buy veal or beef legs. It would take me a day to remove the hair left on the skin. I would cover them with water and salt in order to clean them. Then I would put them in a large pot and would cook them in water with a lot of garlic. The big pot would cook on a slow fire, which was our sole means of cooking. We used petrol. I had to wake up many times at night to check and see if there was enough water left in the pot or that there was enough petrol. This would cook all the night and the next day until noon. We would buy special bread called *sangak*, which was baked over hot pebbles. My sister, brothers, their families and friends would join us for this noon meal. Men drank vodka and women tea. We ate black radishes with this food. Everybody would praise my cooking, but deep in my heart I knew they were able to do what I was doing, only they did not want to go through the hard work. When we finished eating, I had to heat hot water to wash the dishes with soap. Sometimes they would stay to help me and sometimes they had to hurry back home.

By this time I had become more aware. I knew each one's thoughts and it did not bother me to see how they were flattering me in order to take advantage of me. It was not evil, it was human and I accepted it. Regardless, I still enjoyed seeing all my remaining family gathered together. I would tell myself that their presence was a blessing and we had to cherish these moments that were given us. I also had the responsibility to pass our family love and traditions to my grandchildren. Regardless of all, when we lost our father, Nicola took over. When I lost Yeprem and my house, my brother and his wife came to my aid. There is always a price to pay for everything. Family ties have been an important part of our tradition and I tried to pass it to my family. Our grandchildren called our sister and brothers, aunt and uncle and their children were very close to each other. I was the only grandmother for our entire family, which was okay with me.

Women were emancipated in Iran. They were going to schools, and universities. Some had started working out of their homes in real jobs. I was witnessing all these changes, but it was too late for me to take advantage of these opportunities. I was tied to my everyday life. So I hoped that my grandchildren would study and achieve in life.

Hrayr was growing into a handsome young man. Unfortunately he was not very drawn to studying. He started working although none of us were happy. We begged him to study, but it did not help. He promised that when he collected enough money, he would migrate to the United States and study there. But soon he decided to marry and again we thought that he was repeating the same error. He chose his destiny and lived with its consequences. After he and his wife migrated to the United States, I missed him a lot. I only saw him and his family once.

My only joy and hope remained with RoseMary. She did what I had wanted to do what I expected my daughter and Hrayr to do. She studied and was an excellent student. I bought her lollipops whenever she became the first in her class. There was a shop not far from my sister's house that had large American lollipops wrapped in silver foil with colored dots. The color showed the flavor of the candy, green for lime, yellow for lemon and pink for cherry. I would buy her only one and she would work very hard all year to earn these candies. While we would walk home from the candy shop, it would take us more than half an hour. Delicately, she sucked on the lollipop, enjoying it until the wooden stick appeared. Then she would talk to me about the next flavor that she chose next semester. Once at home she would flatten the foil that had covered the candy between the pages of her book and continues to study.

She did oil painting, played the piano and studied her lessons and languages. I listened to the classical pieces she played. Although I knew nothing about this type of music, somehow deep in my heart I felt I had heard them before, and I enjoyed the music. She talked to me about everything she did. She took me to see movies or sights in the city. When the king or the queen visited, she took me to watch them in their cars. On occasion, she bought me little gifts. I enjoyed seeing her grow up.

RoseMary finished high school and started college. She had friends of all religions, Assyrians, Moslems, Jews, Bahais and Zoroastrians. I was still uncomfortable seeing her with some of these friends. But she would say, "We all look alike. What is the difference?" She was right. I did not want to give her the prejudices that I had. I was hoping that time had changed and people were respecting each other more for what they were and not for their beliefs. She participated in exhibitions, concerts and traveled in the country. I would go with her wherever she would invite us and I was proud of her achievements. When she graduated from college, it was the happiest day of my life. We took many pictures of her in cap and gown. Bacrate and Liana were also very happy. We had a profound bond. RoseMary told me she had never seen me so proud and happy. I answered her that it was the day I dreamed of and that I was hoping to see her even more successful. Then she left for America and Europe. She traveled and studied abroad, but she never forgot me.

Life had changed and many new products were introduced in our country that made life easier and more comfortable. When RoseMary came back from the United States she brought me little gadgets for cooking that made my work easier. The night of the New Year when we returned home from my sister's house we were shocked to see that she had bought me a gas stove. She showed me how to cook chicken in the broiler and how I could bake a cake in the oven and cook food on the burners. It took me some months to learn how to use my gas stove as I thought that the taste of the food would change because of the high heat. She had learned some new recipes and was showing me how to use the stove. The country's economy was getting better. We went to the first supermarket opened in the city and did our shopping by pushing a little cart. They had all kinds of food and canned foods that I would never buy. There was toilet paper instead of newspapers that people used. We did not argue over the price or the weight. Everything was clearly marked and employees were ready to help and answer questions. Of course, supermarkets were available for the rich people first and then, little by little, expanded to the rest of the population. Then the telephone became more available for people. What a great tool! I never imagined that in Khoy I would see all these changes one day. The telephone and the airplane were the most amazing discoveries.

The King of Iran was Mohammed Reza Shah. He was

young when he became the King. When he married the sister of the King of Egypt, there was much festivity in the city. But their marriage did not last long. Later he remarried Soraya. We watched them on their wedding day, passing in their cars near our house. It was a big event. There were complications because of the oil supplies and the new Prime Minster. One day the Shah and his wife left the country, and there were demonstrations and shouting in the streets. With shootings and civil disorder, I was afraid for everyone's safety. The day when the Shah left, people attacked the government offices and homes of wealthy people. They looted and stole all that they could. Standing in front of our gate I trembled when I saw people carrying typewriters, chairs, and even doors to their houses. I could see them looting our houses in Khoy and I was telling myself that regardless of progress, human nature had not changed much. What were they going to tell their children? Teach them how to steal!

They destroyed all the statues of the King and his father. Then suddenly there was another revolution and the Shah and the Queen returned to the country. Now we could see the same looters. This time they carried the opposition's belongings. The statues were rebuilt, and they went back to their places. We saw many changes in the country. Then there was the dramatic divorce of the King from his Queen, because she was not able to bear a child. It was sad news for the people. We had radios by this time and we listened to the news. Later the King remarried Farah Diba, a young student, in a big wedding with festivities in the city. When she bore their first son, there were celebrations in the city for days. There were fireworks and decorations all over. In declaring the *White Revolution*, the Shah freed the peasants and distributed the lands to them. The country's economy became better. In the villages, even the peasants had radios and some even had televisions. Laundry detergents came on the market. Soft drink factories opened in Iran. When Pepsi Cola came on the market, it was a big event. We all went to visit the factory. Through glass windows, we could see, for the first time, how the bottles were filled automatically. Like little soldiers they were rolled in line, to be capped, labeled and packed. Then Americans walked on the moon. It was amazing. Who would have thought in my lifetime that I could be witnessing both the worst human horrors and the best human achievements?

We also started taking vacations and went to the Caspian Sea. It was dark blue and there were many delicious fresh fish that we could buy and cook. At night the waves would wash high. In spring the air would smell of orange blossoms everywhere. We always had a good time and I enjoyed watching the water and listening to its noise at night. RoseMary swam like a fish, and she would insist that I join her. Finally I started entering the water, enjoying nature.

Life was getting better for everyone. Still there were many poor and uneducated people in the country. As life got better, people became less satisfied. They blamed the existing problems on Americans. The population had grown from eleven million to forty million. Chickens were not grown in the farms as in old days but in incubators. People in the market would say, "Nowadays, chickens don't have any taste. This is the fault of Americans." Cars and buses began filling our streets. When the bad smell of gas offended our noses and lungs, or if we had dry weather or hard rain, they would say, "This is all because of the Americans. They send rockets into the sky and destroy nature." Seeing all the comfort around us, I would ask myself why people did not appreciate what they had. We were happy with so little in the old days. Now we had so much and still were not happy.

RoseMary insisted that we move to a much larger house. It was a big house by Teheran University, near a large boulevard. A new park was opposite our house. We had many rooms and a nice terrace, running hot water and all the comforts. We had to buy gas in tanks. She would tell us that in America and Europe they had the same system, water and the gas would come automatically to their homes. But it was not a big problem. We would call and they would deliver the gas. In summer and until the weather was nice, we would sleep on the terrace under the moonlight. I enjoyed our new house a lot. At night we would talk to our neighbors from terrace to terrace and later we could see that everyone was quiet and asleep. I would look at the clear sky and watch the movements of the moon and the stars and would ask myself where Yeprem was and where my parents and relatives were. Sometimes I would imagine that each star represented one of them. Sometimes I would think that they were hiding behind the moon. I would get tired and my eyes would close and I would wake up with the warm reflection of the rising sun. From our terrace I could see the white snowy top of Mount Alborz, which resembled Mount Ararat. But Alborz, had only one white peak, whereas Ararat had two. When RoseMary was in town she would have parties. She had many friends who would come to our house and I would enjoy seeing them talk, laugh and dance. At night when we would go to bed she would tell jokes and make me laugh. Life was going smoothly, Liana was a successful dressmaker. She owned her own business and had many customers who admired her work.

We kept our traditions, gathering for weddings, birthdays and religious festivities. We would visit each other on New Year's Eve or other major holidays. We shared expenses with my sister and brothers, and we would all prepare a huge turkey for New Year's Eve and eat it with rice and other dishes. To watch our grandchildren playing together was a joy for us. We had done our work and they were the ones who would carry the flame. We would celebrate *Der entaratch* [19], and there was another holiday, *Vardavayr*, when we would gather together and we would throw water on each other and laugh. Then of course we would celebrate the Ascension with a large picnic. Nicola lived in a large farmhouse and we would celebrate this last holiday in his house. We kept some of the traditions of Khoy and taught them to our children and grandchildren. Then there were weddings, childbirth, baptisms and, unfortunately, funerals. All were followed by meals that we would share with each other. Once a week we would visit my sister and the next week she and her family would come and visit us. Nicola worked and traveled with his two sons. In one of his trips he became ill and died in Shiraz, a beautiful city in the mid-south of Iran. His sons buried him there and we held a week of mourning in our house. It was very hard for everyone. He was my dearest brother, friend, and my father. His kind face with his blue eyes had been carved in my heart and memory. I will never forget all that he

---

[19.] When we would burn fires and everyone would jump over them. This Holiday originates from the time when Armenians were Zoroastrians. The fire represents good health. When we jumped over the fire we said: " My pale color to you and your red color will come to my cheeks."

did for us. His love for us was perpetuated through his three children. They have always been kind, loving and respectful to all of us and we have always honored Kharse as the matriarch of our family.

Later my younger brother and his family decided to immigrate to Armenia, which was under Russian power. For all of us it was a sad day, as going to Soviet Armenia in those days was equal to dying. We were not able to communicate with them freely. Letters, telephones and trips were controlled and almost non-existent. My sister and I cried. We begged them not to leave, but his wife was the one who was anxious to leave Iran. She argued that life in Soviet Armenia would be more enriching for her children who were talented and pursuing music and ballet. Maybe she was right as all the Russian propaganda in Iran showed us how they were strong in music, dance and sports. We had two embassies and cultural centers, American and Russian, not far from our house and they showed free propaganda movies and performances. Sometimes people would be attracted by one of them. They left the country and we heard very little from them.

RoseMary traveled abroad again, and she called us often wherever she was. She sent gifts and postcards. Sometimes when I missed her and Hrayr, I would curse the airplane flying above us and curse the inventor of this metal bird that carried my grandchildren so far away. Later she traveled to some conferences in Israel, Germany and France. Then she decided to study at the Sorbonne in Paris for her doctorate degree. Before her departure she taught at the Iranian Air Force base and then at Teheran University. I was proud of her achievements. But one day she came home upset and I learned that she had received an I.D. card in order to enter the base but after nationality they had written: Christian. She was very hurt. "I always considered myself a true Iranian," she said. "But it seems they do not forget that I am not Muslim. They will always remain the same. Why should I spend my entire life in a country where I always would be considered a second class citizen?" They had also proposed that she change her *name* [20] so that she would get higher positions. I felt that this was her final departure from the country that she had loved and served so sincerely. She asked me to visit her in Paris, but she could not see that I was getting ready for another trip. Finally, I had done what I had to do in this world. Now I had but one wish: I was just waiting to hear that she was married and had a child. That was my final wish. I hoped to give my blessings to the child and leave this world forever.

RoseMary was married in Paris to a young Jewish man. For their honeymoon they came to visit us. He was a nice young man. I looked at him and told myself, "Why have people killed and massacred us for our religious beliefs and because of our differences? See how these two young love-birds are happy together. What is the difference between humans? We all come from one source and return to the same source. Why have others not learned this? Could not we accept each other like these two young couple and live together in peace? They stayed with us for two weeks and traveled around the country. We ate and talked together but I held back. I was leaving her the freedom, to build a new life of her own.

They left Iran and, as always, I hugged and kissed her. She

---

[20] - Meaning to convert to Islam.

looked at me and our spirits spoke together. I heard that she told her mother to watch over me because I would not live long. She knew, but she left, as she had to continue her life. She had to finish her degree and she knew what I was expecting from her. Some months later she gave us the good news that they were expecting a baby. I had always told her that I would like to hear that she had a baby, then I could die peacefully. On the ninth month, Liana went to be with her daughter for the birth of her grandchild. I refused to accompany her as I was getting ready for my final trip. When Ishac, RoseMary's husband called and announced that Mabelle was born on the first of September, I knew that I had accomplished my goals. I had done all that I had to do. My body started preparing the release of my spirit. It became weaker and weaker. Bacrate was very sad. He always loved and respected me like his own mother. He always appreciated my presence and my help. He called Paris to announce that I was ill. Liana rushed back to Iran. RoseMary sent a pair of little white mittens for me that they had put on Mabelle's hands so that she would not scratch her face with her little nails. I smelled and kissed these little gloves and told Liana not to cry for me as Mabelle had come to replace me.

I had nothing more to do in this world. It seemed to me that I had achieved some of my goals and now Yeprem was waiting for me. I was eager to see him again and find my eternal peace. I blessed everyone and closed my eyes with a smile. Now I could see Yeprem clearly, without the presence of the Turkish soldiers and without blood, smiling at me, like the day of our wedding. It was telling me that all would be just fine. He took my cold hands in his large warm hands. Suddenly I felt their warmth blanketing with love and strength. While we were holding hands, we looked down and saw Liana and Bacrate in tears over my deserted body, but we knew that they would recover later. I looked at my body left under the white sheets on the bed and felt pity for this tired body that had to go through so much in such a short journey. Now I was going to join the real source. I was remembering all the experiences of my life on earth. I was leaving completely empty-handed.

As soon as Liana and the family left my body for the mortuary, a young nurse looked around. When she saw the hallway was clear, she approached my finger where I still had the turquoise ring. She pulled it off my finger. I again looked at the empty house that had sheltered me until this day. I asked my empty body to forgive the last acts of the humans. I thanked her for carrying my soul and all the problems of this world so patiently. Yeprem pulled me gently, and then a strong light appeared in front of us, showing us the path of eternity. I felt the warmth and I heard the familiar melodies of the prayers. Then I felt completely weightless. A strong joy filled my spirit. Finally I had found the real peace that I had been looking for my entire life.

THE END

POSTSCRIPT

❧

A year before my grandmother died, she gave me a little colorful hat and told me that it was the only object which was left from her past. My grandfather had worn it on their wedding day. He had told her that his great grandmother had sewn and decorated this hat and he was wearing it as a symbol in order to invite the presence of their spirits for such a joyous day. I was surprised she had kept this keepsake from us. She said she hoped God would forgive her for this. Kharse had stolen the hat from her, and she had never wanted to give it back to her. It had a great sentimental value for my grandmother, but for others it had only monetary value, because it is, quite an amazing piece all sewn by hand. A long time ago she had seen the hat in the house of Kharse's daughter, so she had stolen it back. My grandmother never cared for all the gold and jewelry that she had lost. But this little hat was different. I have treasured it. When my older son became *bar mitzvah*, I put it on his head and said it was a gift from his great grandparents that he has never met. It fit him perfectly and I am sure that God has forgiven my grandmother to take back what belonged to her originally.

The second object I have in my possession is a piece of gold with the picture of Tsar Nicola on it. When we married and went to visit my parents, Nicola's oldest son came to see us. He gave us a red box. He said that it was a gift from his mother, Kharse, and him for our wedding. Later, when I opened the box and showed the golden piece to my grandmother, she smiled sadly and said, "Surprise! This is one of my gold pieces. At least you have one of them in your hand now."

A WORD ABOUT SOME SURVIVORS

છ&

From a very big city where many hundreds of Armenian families lived, these are the only survivors. With all their memories shared, somehow the remaining generation's children have kept a close relationship with each other. After all, none of us have a complete family like most people, who have grandparents, aunts and uncles. Our family size is reduced because of the massacre. Our parents' conflicts during and after the massacre did not affect us. We are not here to judge each other. As a teenager, when I learned all the dirty secrets of our family, I got very upset for the injustices that my grandmother and mother had suffered. After many years, I understood why my grandmother forgave everyone. She loved and visited them and never talked about the past. After many years, they all died and are buried in the same size lot. No one took anything with them. But their memories and love has perpetuated in our spirits.

As a child I used to see the large tree with the storks on it in my daydreams. I dreamed of my grandfather's horse and their colorful snake. I heard the clear music of the waterfall in the mountains. I never dreamed of the jewelry that my grandmother had. I can see those gems in stores and museums all over the world; they are just cold stones. I do not care that we did not receive them as a heritage from our ancestors. But the unconditional love of my grandmother has followed me all over the world. It has given me the strength that I needed to go on through difficult moments of my life. Her courage has sustained me; her smile has given me energy to do all that I have done. The Turks killed our families and stole our belongings, but they could not take the God-given gifts from the souls of the survivors. Arousiak loved us, and she burned like a candle to enlighten us, hoping that we would make this world a better place. She hoped that no one would ever experience what she and her people had endured.

The Survivors

৵

After the revolution of Khomeini in Iran, many Iranians left the country. Among them were a few of the survivors or the children of the survivors who left Iran for Europe and for the United States of America, and again they started a new life.

These are the only survivors that I have met with or knew in Iran.

৵

GHOUKAS KARAPETIAN

Ghoukas, like most of the survivors, moved with her mother and two sisters to Teheran after World War II. We used to visit each other once in awhile. Ghoukas had a store on the main boulevard and used to make keys and sell lock and supplies. He wrote some articles in Armenian. He married late, but did not have children.

His mother lived with him, and both died in Iran. His younger sister now lives in Teheran with her children.

His older sister, **Vartanoush**, lived with her daughter in North Hollywood, California. Her son lives in Australia. Both of her children are married and have children. Vartanoush died in August of 2001. She is buried in Forest Lawn in Burbank,California.

151

The Survivor

NAZAN TARO ESTEPANIAN

Nazan lives in Glendale, California, with her younger daughter. She has an older daughter and a son whose name is Andranik. Her mother-in-law, Banafsheh, had named him after the Armenian soldier Andranik, because she never forgot what she had seen that night in the city gathering especially the cross on his chest.

Her older daughter and her two grandsons and their families also live in Glendale, California. The irony is that the younger daughter, a very attractive girl who grew up in Teheran, fell in love with a Muslim boy and as her parents would not permit her to marry him, she ran away and married him anyway. She has a handsome son who also lives in Glendale, California.

❧

NASIK STEPANIAN

Nasik married and had a daughter. Her husband died young. She lived with her daughter who married and has a son who is married and has a child. Nasik died in Iran. Her daughter, his son and his family live in Iran. Nasik's younger sister, Vartoush, has a son who is married and has a daughter. They live in Iran. Vartoush is still alive, but she does not recognize anyone anymore.

❧

The Survivor

MRS. SARDARIAN *and his son* GHEVOND LEON

I met a man who works in a market in West Los Angeles. It is rare to see an Armenian working in that part of the city. His name is Leon. One day while I was talking to him, I asked him where he was from. He told me that his parents were from Khoy. I was amazed to meet someone from Khoy. I asked his mother's name and later I told my mother about him. She knew his mother in Iran and said that they had visited each other. When I asked Leon if he remembered anything about the massacre, he said that his mother never talked about the massacre. She would only say that they were very young when the Turks took their father and they crossed the wheat field, which was in front of their house where they were hiding, to reach the famous mountain where all the men were taken. She said that while they were crossing the field, the soldiers shot her father from behind. He fell down, but then he stood up; after a minute the soldiers shot him, and again he stood up. But the third time they shot him he never got up. And always she would cry and say it was horrible. He told me this was all that he knew about her past. She would speak of it with such heavy tears, so he stopped asking her questions.

ॐ

The Survivor

NAZAN KARAPETIAN

Nazan had two daughters, both married. The younger daughter had a son. Her husband died young. She worked hard and took care of her only son but he died at a young age, and much later she died in Iran. The older daughter had two daughters, who are married. The younger daughter has two daughters. Their mother died in Iran but Nazan came to America after the Khomeini revolution in Iran, when she was in her late nineties. Her older grandchild took very good care of her. We went to visit her in Glendale. It was nice to see her, as she was the oldest survivor. How could one think that after all those hard times, she would finally come to live in the United States? At the end of her life she was not able to recognize anyone but three days before her death, she spoke only in Turkish. She was repeating, "Agha, Agha [21], take my shoes but please give me back my child. Agha, take my money, take our house, but please leave my children alone. Agha, take all I have, take all you want, but please don't harm my children. Agha, Agha..." On the third day she died while still talking to Agha. She is buried in Glendale, California.

❧

---

[21]- Sir in Iranian, but it was also the name of the person with whom she stayed.

NICOLA AND VARTOUHI MIHRANIAN

Nicola and Kharse died in Iran, Nicola from cancer in Shiraz. He was the patriarch of our family, a very kind and beautiful person. His death touched our entire family. For my grandmother, her sister and brother the death of their brother was very hard. Vartouhi died in her late nineties from old age. She lived her last years comfortably in a nice house that her children had prepared for her. We visited her often and I always thought that she was still the most advanced thinker of our family. In the last years of her life, she would always say that there were people who were stealing her belongings. Their older son, Mihran, married very late, her daughter Miranda lives with her mother in Teheran, Iran. He died from a heart attack some years before his mother. They never told Vartouhi that his son had died, but we knew that she had understood, as she would say; "How come he does not come to visit me? He has never stayed away for so long on his trips." Their daughter, Lousik married and has three children, Vigen, Sylva and Ida, and three grandchildren, She lives in Switzerland but also travels to England and Iran, depending on where her children live. Their youngest son, Ashot, married and had two children, Yeprem and Maria. His wife and their children and three grandchildren, live in the United States. He died in Iran some years ago from a heart attack. We met him in California several months before his death, and I could see that the strong handsome boy had turned into a weak old man.

છ

ZAROUHI MEHRANIAN

Zarouhi and her husband lived and died in Iran. They had three children. Her older son, Sahak (Norik), married and had three daughters Meline, Emeline and Tenny. He died some years ago from a heart attack. Their youngest daughter fell in love with a Muslim boy and married him. His widow, their daughters and the four grand children live in Iran.

Zarouhi's daughter, Maryam, is married and has two sons, Hakop and Harmik. They live with their sons and four grand-children in Toronto, Canada.

Their youngest son, Sarkis, lives with his wife and son, Artin in Glendale, California.

ॐ

AGHASI AND HASMIK MEHRANIAN

Aghasi and his wife lived in Iran with their three children, a daughter, Sanam, and two sons, Henrik and Edward. Later they immigrated to Armenia. They lived there and had another son, Ashot. They then moved to the United States. His wife and the four children, and their grandchildren, Arman, Edgar, Inessa, and their two great grand children live in Glendale and in North Hollywood, California. We met Aghasi several times. I was happy that at least my children had a chance to meet the brother of their great grandmother. He died of old age and is buried in Burbank, California.

ॐ

LIANA YEPREMI HAYRAPETIAN - HAROUTUNIAN

Liana is the only surviving daughter of Arousiak and Yeprem. After the death of her husband Bacrate (Bagrat), she moved to Paris and lived with her daughter's family. Later she migrated to the United States.

Liana lives in West Hollywood, California, with her son, Hrayr. He has two daughters, Melinda and Evelina who work and live in Los Angeles.

Her daughter, RoseMary lives with her husband Ishac in Los Angeles. Their children, Mabelle, Ruben and Elia, are at graduate schools in different states. Their daughter, Liana, is buried in Mount Sinai Cemetery in Burbank, California.

Bibliography

&

For us, Khoy was a word from past, not a city. We only knew that our grandparents lived there and then after the Armenian massacre my grandmother and mother left their belongings and their past life behind in Khoy. The city of Khoy was buried in the cemetery of our minds.

Wrong !

I had just finished my manuscript that a friend told me about a book named **The History of Khoy by Dr. Mohamad Amin Riahi, published in 2000 by Tarh-e No in Tehran - Iran (in Farsi), 602 pages.** Dr. Amin Riahi who is a native of Khoy has put fifty years of his life doing research on his beloved city.

When I read this book I felt that the city of Khoy has emerged from the dust of past memory. I could find some descriptions and events that corresponded to the information that I had gathered from the survivors. Although I have not seen this beautiful city now I have special feelings for it. The pictures in the book gave me the opportunity to ask myself and wonder how my grandparent's houses and environments looked like. How their friends and neighbors looked and it also inspired me to paint some oil paintings in order to re-establish our family album, which was buried in my grandparent's garden. By doing so I found a new peace within myself and I could see appreciation and clearance of memory in my mothers' eyes. Just by looking at these paintings, many dark and forgotten memories and answers came back to my mother and me. While painting, for the first time in my life I felt that I was not alone, there were forces present within me helping.

I do not know Dr. Riahi personally but I thank him for this wonderful book that he has accomplished. He is the only person that I know of who has mentioned honestly the massacre of the Armenians of Khoy and the neighboring cities and villages. He even mentions that these people lived there for centuries and were integrated in Persian society and there was no good reason to exterminate them. Here I have only translated some passages that I feel add additional information to the true story of *The Survivor.*

෴

The city of Khoy is situated in the Northwest of Iran in the State of Azarbaijan. Khoy has a history of 2700 years. It is one of the most prosper and "green" cities of Iran. Water is abundant and it has a very clean and pleasant air.

Mount Aurin is situated in Khoy. Its highest altitude is 3550 meters. Its peak is always covered with snow in winter, as well as in summer.

The origin of the name Khoy is not known. Some say it comes from the Armenian word meaning, "migrate." Others think that it is originated from Pahlavi roots, meaning salt. Actually we can find salt mines not very far from Khoy. Khoy has been situated on the East-West trading road, known as the Silk Road.

There is a water source in Khoy that is warm in winter and cold in summer. The river of Salsabil runs through the city. There are many waterfalls and pure water sources, which run from the depths of the mountains.

Khoy is also situated on a seismic line; there have been some major earthquakes in this city that caused much damage to the buildings and had killed many people.

Many foreign visitors like the American priest, Wilson, who had visited Khoy in 1881. Jobere who was sent by Napoleon lived in Khoy. Mr. Barnard a French engineer who died in Khoy is buried in the Armenian cemetery, all compared the city of Khoy to Paradise.

The existing mountains in Khoy and the importance of its geographical situation has been one of the reasons for their different conflicts and wars. In peacetime it had been a reason for thieves to attack merchants and travelers in *gardaneh*[22] of these mountains. This is the main reason that many *Caravansaries* were build around and in the city to accommodate the travelers. Many of the travelers would stay there for extra days in order to join others, to make a bigger caravan so that the thieves would find it harder to attack.

There is a large boulevard in the middle of the city, which is about two miles long. Large and small rivers run in its borders. This boulevard ends with a white wall where the tower of the city is located. Many old weeping willows are planted side by side along the water. The gardens do not have high walls. Fruit trees are abundant in the city, especially mulber-

---

[22]. The pass.

ry and apricot trees can be seen everywhere. The city is covered with the perfume of myriad red roses. Even to this day, the roses of Khoy are in demand in the market because of their beauty and fragrance. In spring, the smell of the perfume of flowers like roses, tulips, hyacinths and other flowers and herbs cover the valleys around the city, which is situated on a very fertile land. The quality of the soil and the abundance of water have helped in the production of its main exports, like cotton, rice, dried fruits, grapes, wheat and barley. They used to say that the wheat and barely grains of Khoy are larger and its fruits are more juicy and delicious than anywhere else in the country.

They used to export oil, skins and other animal products as well as dried fruits to many countries and especially to Russia and instead, they would import garments and everyday products back to Khoy. Later the habitants of Khoy learned the art of weaving. They made thread and started manufacturing fabrics in Khoy. The silkworms have been grown in Khoy and the woven silk fabrics existed in the market until fifty years ago. Persian rugs from Khoy are much in demand. The gold of Khoy was known for its quality and purity. The hand- carved brass objects are still famous.

There were many towers that could be seen in the distance. Its *bazaar*, tower and gates are shaped like a cross, facing each other. The Carevansara, *bazaar*, post and telegraph offices are well built. In the period of the Quajar dynasty, there were four gates, twenty mosques and six *Hamams*. The Khan *hamam* [23] and its pool were built of marble. The Khan

---

[23]- Bathhouse.

Bazaar was built with white stones. Later columns and *Gonbads* [24] were added to it. There are 10.000 houses with 50.000 in population. The *Masjede Jomeh* [25] was built in 1899 C.E. Some Armenian craftsmen who were known for their skill in carving stones were asked to work in the construction of the mosque, which caused some conflicts among the Moslems. The opposition had said that they have used Christians to build a Moslem mosque. The *Mohamad Beil Hamam* can still be found in Khoy. The *Shish Cheshmeh* [26] is built on the Ghatour River three kilometers south of Khoy in the valley of the Ghazanfar Mountains. Khoy was divided into different sections known as Tagh.

The garden of Delgosha, is situated in the valley of the mountains. The garden is surrounded by very old trees and covered with flowers. There are small lakes and large pools in this beautiful garden.

Jobere says that the population of Khoy is about 25,000 people. They are good-looking, with white skin and fine features. They seem more educated and advanced than their neighboring Turks, Ottomans do.

There were many rich landlords who lived in Khoy. They owned many lands, and the peasants who worked for them. As Khoy had very pleasant weather, many famous personalities would come there from the capital to enjoy life in summers. They would give large parties and invite many guests. The Crown Prince of Quajar used to pass his time in Khoy hunting, travelling and enjoying the women of his *Haramsera* [27].

---

24. Domes.
25. Friday Mosque.
26. Six-water source.
27. Harem.

The oldest existing building in Khoy is the Sourp Sarkis Church. Its original construction date is not known but it is believed that the Armenian documents prove that this church was built in the year 332-333. Near the entrance door on a red stone one can read the date of 1120 carved on it. In Armenian documents it shows that the last restorations dated is the year 1620. It is situated in the village of Mahlehzan, seventeen kilometers Northwest of Khoy. Mr. Wilson writes that on one of its walls he had recognized a painting that shows the Roman Emperor Constantine and his wife Helena.Sourp Sarkis Church is 32 meters long and 18 meters large. The thickness of the stone walls are estimated one and half meter. The length of the walls from outside is about five meters. The floor of the church is deeper than its usual levelas centuries of flood, earthquake and other elements witness the old age of this building.

The people of Khoy have gone through many hard times during their existence. They have suffered from natural and human created tragedies. Many strong earthquakes have destroyed villages and killed many people. Wars and conflicts have damaged the city and its population. History has rolled and the people have changed faces, but the human tragedies have continued.

In the years 1904-1906 C.E.an epidemic of cholera was spread in Khoy which killed many people. In 1907 another epidemic of cholera was spread in Khoy, although many people died from it, this time it was a little milder.

Many wars and conflicts existed since the time of the Maad Dynasty. I am only referring to the period closer to the Armenian massacre.

During 1214 most of the soldiers who were in the Quajar

army were men from different tribes, whose aims were only based on the possibility of looting and stealing from the population.

The political situation has not been calm for a long period. The Constitutional Revolutionists formed forces in different cities and started their opposition against the central government. From 1898 the revolution of Khoy has started because of the influence of the Social Democratic ideas, coming from Europe, and especially Russia. The existing peasant and landlord situation in Iran and the intrigues of foreign interest in the region had helped to the existence of all these troubles. The peasants learned to say that the land should belong to the person who works on it.

During these periods not only Armenians but many Muslim Iranians of Khoy were killed. In one of the attacks, Azukhan, who was a very cruel, brutal, blood seeker man, killed many people [28].

During all these turbulence the Armenians of Khoy have stayed loyal to their city and even they have helped and fought with them side by side.

Haydar Khan had asked the Armenian Priest of Koy and their *Fedayees* for help. The Armenians brought him the Armenian *Fedayee* uniform and rescued him as an Armenian and saved his life [29].

Another example is that in earlier times there was a meeting that took place between the Iranian Mojahedeen of Khoy, in the presence of the Turkish Ottoman, Khail Beig and many of the Armenians Fedaees were present as well [30].

---

[28]. pp.424, ibid
[29]. pp.433, ibid
[30]. pp.438, ibid.

Bibliography

On one side there were the presence of the local opposition towards the central government and on the other side there were the fighting that was taking place between the Russians and the Turks. On each occasion the innocent Armenian population suffered. "The Russians forced 6000 Armenian families from neighboring villages and cities to move to Russia. It is written that with their departure some of the Armenian villages of Khoy and Salmas were destroyed and the economy of the region dropped because of this departure" [31].

A German craftsman established an orphanage and was teaching in Khoy. Later people learned that the presence of this German citizen had a political origin rather a humanitarian act.

During the fights between Russians and Turks, their armies crossed the two main city of Khoy and Salmas which caused a lot of damage and loss to these cities. Thus many Armenians and Persians were killed because of these conflicts and while the Russian soldiers stayed in Khoy they burned the *bazaar* and rubbed people.

The Iranian and Armenian *Mojahedeen* were fighting for political freedom and other ideologies with their central government, side by side. On each occasion the Turkish government was taking advantage of different situations to attack neighboring villages and cities and was killing the Armenian population. In one occasion while the army of Khoy was busy fighting in the city of Salmas as the Russians had become weaker in the war with Turcks, the Turks took the advantage to attack all the local Armenian population of

---

[31]- pp.333, ibid.

Van and the neighboring cities. Many women and children who were able to flee this massacre and walked heading to Nakhjevan in Armenia. When they were approaching Khoy in the vally of Ghotour, they asked the permission of the authorities to stay for a few days in Khoy in order to give a chance to the elderly and children to rest. But the local authorities refused their demand and added, if they approached the city they would all be shot to death. Simitghou was sent by the local government to destroy the constitutional Revolutionists. He was a very cruel person. In the spring of 1918, he learned about these Armenian refugees. Simitghou and his soldiers surrounded the Armenians in the valley of Ghotour and till the evening he killed so many of them that the river of Ghotour changed its blue color to their red blood. Then he collected all their belongings and gathered the rest of the captured to Khoy. The next day he ordered hi soldiers to kill all of them in front of the *Emamzadehe* [32] in Peer Valley, he even killed the Muslim priest authority, the *Mojtahed* of the city [33].

In April after another confrontation many Armenian refugees arrived to Khoy, they were estimated to be 4000 people. Simitghou attacked these refugees, stole and killed many of them. From the other side the Kurds and Turks killed the remaining Armenians. Because of the non-existing hygienic situation, the remaining people contracted plague and died from it, and another epidemics started in Khoy for the general population.

In May of 1918 the Turkish military started arriving to

---

[32]- A monument built on the birthplace of a prophet.
[33]- pp.472, ibid.

Khoy. At the beginning 24 soldiers and one trumpet blower arrived to Khoy. Two days later more of them arrived and soon their number added to 700 soldiers. They were from the sixth troup of the Turkish army.

In May 1918 General Andranik, the Armenian general, with his 5,000 strong army men, came to Khoy to face the Turks who had just conquered Salmas and were holding a big party. First he was welcomed with the local authorities. But later many Turks started spreading anti-Armenian rumors in the city, saying that they should not trust the Armenians. They said that the Armenian soldiers were cutting the Moslem captured soldiers, into pieces and eating them. This type of false propaganda turned the Muslim population against the Christians. The Turks immediately, even before Andranik arrived, went to different villages and started killing the Armenian population-adults and children. Then they surrounded the village of Var, which was about 6 kilometers away from Khoy. Its population was mostly composed of Armenians. They attacked from all sides and killed all the men, women and children and stole all their belongings. A part of this population was composed of the Armenian refugees who were spared from the massacre of Turkey and had come to Iran for protection [34].

In the beginning, Andranik advanced and attacked the Turks, but then more Turkish soldiers and artilleries arrived and Andranik was obliged to move back and cross the Araks River burning the bridge behind him. Unfortunately after their departure the Turkish soldiers started cleansing all the surrounding villages of Iran from Armenian population.

---

[34] - pp.400, ibid

In the middle of the night, the Turkish soldiers searched Armenians every where. They pulled out all the Armenians who were hiding in their houses and in their Muslim friend's houses, they took them all out of the city and killed them without pity. All the men and boys over age of ten years were automatically killed.

Although Khoy was spared from another war, the consequences of these massacres destroyed the local economy, famine and sickness spread in the city, which killed many thousands of people [35].

In all these events, two-third of the population of Khoy died. From 40.000 refugee population of Salmas, not even 10.000 were saved. The Turks were gathering all the corpses from mosques, houses and the streets and were putting them in a carriage, and they buried them without prayers and respect for the death in the common ditches. The Muslim people of Khoy suffered a lot and as Mola Jafar, a Muslim priest writes in his memories: "The population is suffering because of the actions and the injustices of Turkish Asgars [36]. They steal all that they see, they robe people. They take their horses from the people on the roads. They confiscate all the fruits from the farms and gardens. They even kill who they please." The population of Khoy became more isolated and pulled back to themselves. They closed their doors where neighbors did not have news from each other [37].

These horrors are explained honestly and in details for the first time in this book. I am not going to refer to all of the atrocities. It seems that the assassination of my grandfather

---

[35]- pp.479, ibid
[36]- Soldiers.
[37]- pp.480, ibid.

corresponds to the final massacre of the Armenians of Khoy, which took place in June of 1918. So we learned for the first time that the day that my grandfather was killed corresponds to the third birthday of my mother. When I told my mother about this, I asked her: " I am sure as a three-year-old child, you should have some memories of that awful day." By looking sadly at one of my paintings she answered, that now she understands why she has always been afraid of horses. Once when she did a pilgrimage to a holy mountain in Iran every one rode horses and mules but she was one of the rare people who climbed the mountain all the day on foot. Now she asked me to change the background color of the painting of her father. She has never liked bright colors, specially the color red. It is interesting to see how human minds function. In order to protect us from atrocities, sometimes our brain is able to close its doors to unwanted information and store them far away in one of the lost sections of the brain. But now I learned again that do not fade and they do not disappear. They are always present and manifest in their own way, unless we affront them one day and push the delete button with our fingers.

Ə🖐

The Survivor

I would like to refer to some passages of the book:
Ambassador Morgenthau's Story, by Henry Morgenthau [38].

❧

The Sultans' proclamation was an official public document. It says, " He who kills even one unbeliever of those who rule over us, whether he does it secretly or openly, shall be rewarded by God. And let every Moslem, in whatever part of the world he may be, swear a solemn oath to kill at least three or four of the infidels who rule over him, for they are the enemies of God and the faith. Let every Moslem know that his reward for doing so shall be doubled by the God who created heaven and earth."

"Little holy war," the battle which every Mohammedan is to wage in his community against his Christian neighbors [39].
The believers are told to organize, in bands, and to go forth and slay Christians [40].

---

[38]- Gomidas Institute, Ann Arbor. Michigan 2000, 277 pages.
[39]- pp.110, ibid.
[40]- pp.111, ibid.

171

Bibliography

Some passages from the book: ***The Armenians of Iran*** [41].

❧

At the turn of the century, Tabriz was a national Center for the Armenians in northwestern Iran who were involved in trades, crafts and agriculture [42].

In fact, it was the Dashnak group in Tabriz, that in April 1892 called for the first General Congress of the Armenian Revolution Dashnak centers in Iran was in Khoy, Salmas, and Tabriz [43].

We had barely forgotten the horrible massacre of Salmas, Maku and Khoi [44].

Of the Persian Armenians, it is generally estimated that 85 per cent are Gregorians and ten per cent Uniates. The remaining five percent are Protestants, members of the Armenian Evangelical Church, the result largely of Armenian missionary endeavor during the last century in the Ottoman Empire and northwestern Persia. In the latter group are included about 500 Seventh Day Adventists.

One may, consequently, wonder at the temerity of Gregorian Archbishop MelikTangian of Tabriz, strong Dashnakist, in even aspiring to the still vacant patriarchal throne at Etchmiadzin, century old seat, now in Soviet Armenia, of the Armenian Catholicus [45].

---

[41]- Edited by Cosroe Chaqueri, 1998, President and followers of Harvard College. 409 pp.
[42]- pp. 13, ibid.
[43]- pp. 78, ibid.
[44]- pp. 294, ibid.
[45]- pp. 374, ibid.

The Survivor

In the book of
General Andranik and the
Armenian Revolutionary Movement [46].
There are some passages about the events in Khoy:

❧

Immediately after the First World War broke out on July 28, 1914 Andranik sent word to Constantinople that all Armenian revolutionaries and intellectuals should leave the city and go abroad. Unfortunately they did not listen to the hero, who later wrote in his memories, "Men who had been like lions were taken to the slaughterhouse like sheep [47]."

At the time of the incident, Andranik's regiment was encamped near a village called Duzeduz, south of Khoi [48].

Andranik declared, "I have no ill will toward nor any grudges against the peaceful Turkish population. I am fighting only against the Begs and the government. I am not a racist. I recognize only one nation-the nation of oppressed people [49]."

On the morning of June 20, 1918, the Special Striking Division began moving southward through northern Persia. A captive Turkish soldier revealed that the Turks had twelve thousand men in Northern Persia. About twenty miles from Khoi, Andranik had his first clash with enemy troops. With his four hundred cavalrymen he chased the Turks who fled, leaving behind one cannon and a large number of dead [50].

---

46. Antranig Chalabian, USA 1988, 588 pp.
47. pp. 217, ibid.
48. When Kalentarov, archeologist, was in prison. Pp.235, ibid.
49. pp.277, ibid.
50. pp.418, ibid.

Continuing his advance, Andranik reached Seyidavar, an Armenian village eight or nine miles from Khoi [51].

The Armenian Special Striking Division approached the city of Khoi. On Sunday, June 23,1918, General Andranik decided to storm the City.

The Persian leaders of the city came to Andranik, greeted him, and expressed their willingness to submit to him. The Turks' resistance was weak and their artillery ineffective. Until noon, victory summed to be within the Armenians' reach. However, in the afternoon the Turks received substantial help from infantrymen and artillery men called in from Sheitan-Avan and Dizadiz [52].

Toward the June of 1918 finally the Special Striking Divison and the refugees walked all night and made it back to the bridge over the Araxes river. He ordered his cavalrymen to cross to the Russian side and resist the enemy. This was the exact moment that the remaining of the Armenian population in Khoy was massacred for the last time ending the assassination of my grandfather Yeprem.

છ

[51]- pp.419, ibid
[52]- pp.420, ibi

The Map of Armenia, Iran and Turkey

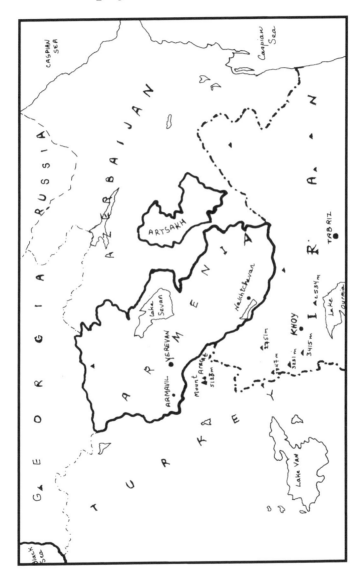

These original oil paintings were inspired by the story of The Survivor, and painted by RoseMary Cohen in Summer of 2001. Paintings number 2, 3, 4 and 12 were inspired by and adapted from The History of Khoy, and painting number 6 from Larousse of Animals.

1- Sweet childhood. (20"x24")

2- Saint Sarkis. (24"x36")

3- Looking inside Saint Sarkis. (20"x24")

4-The main sanctuary - Saint Sarkis. (20"x24")

5- The wedding. (20"x24")

6- The stork family. (24"x36")

7- Yeprem on his white horse. (24"x36")

8- The pregnant victim. (19"x24")

9- The eye of consciousness. (30"x40")

10- The white horse is the witness. (24"x36")

11- Toward a new destiny. (24"x36")

12 - The oldest gate of Khoy. (23"x28")

About the author

ॐ

RoseMary H. Cohen received a Doctorate degree in Sociology from the Sorbonne in Paris. She moved with her family to Los Angeles in 1984. She has owned and operated Atelier de Paris, an international art business since 1985. She has published many articles in different magazines. This is her third book published in the United States.

ALSO BY DR. ROSEMARY H. COHEN

LE DEVELOPPEMENT RURAL: ATTITUDES DES PAYSANS

IRANIENS APRES LA REFORME AGRAIRE

KORBAN- THE SACRIFICE OF LIANA

WATER ART